Praise for *The Taste of Apple Seeds*

"Beautifully ... sometimes ingenious. ...
The Taste of Apple Seeds is atmospheric and sensual. ...
Hagena ingrains the creaking old house—and the book—
with melancholy; every word, every place is weighted with
memories." —*The Independent*

"Hagena's sensitivity and attention to detail, and a narrator
whose honesty and comical clumsiness keep the story light
and engaging, have universal appeal." —*Sunderland Echo*

"*The Taste of Apple Seeds* is a pure masterpiece."
—*Le Nouvel Observateur*

"[Hagena] immerses us in the destiny of three generations
of women. ... Between the lines, you smell the odor of
apples and old stones ... [the author] gives life to memories
in a style whose graveness touches always right. You eat her
apple entirely, even with the apple seeds." —*Elle*

"The author constructs a narration of perfect unity ... with
these different lives that are all intimately connected to
each other." —*Le Monde des Livres*

"It is about heritage, about the weight of the past, a saga
about three generations of women where happiness and
tragedy, humor and gravity mix. ... It is a book of high
sensibility." —Martin Fabre, www.lechoixdeslibraires.com

EAGLE VA
P.O. BOX
EAGLE, C

D1013998

COUNTY LIBRARY DISTRICT
BURLINGTON, IA
51001 — (910) 355-5800

The Taste of Apple Seeds

The Taste of Apple Seeds

Katharina Hagena

TRANSLATED BY JAMIE BULLOCH

WILLIAM MORROW
An Imprint of HarperCollins*Publishers*

This book is a work of fiction. The characters, incidents, and dialogue
are drawn from the author's imagination and are not to be construed as real.
Any resemblance to actual events or persons, living or dead, is entirely coincidental.

First published in Germany in 2008 by Kiepenheuer & Witsch Verlag, GmbH & Co. KG.
First published in Great Britain in 2013 by Atlantic Books, an imprint of Atlantic Books Ltd.

THE TASTE OF APPLE SEEDS. Copyright © 2008 by Katharina Hagena.
Translation copyright © 2013 by Jamie Bulloch. All rights reserved.
Printed in the United States of America. No part of this book may be used
or reproduced in any manner whatsoever without written permission except in the case
of brief quotations embodied in critical articles and reviews. For information address
HarperCollins Publishers, 10 East 53rd Street, New York, NY 10022.

HarperCollins books may be purchased for educational, business, or sales promotional use.
For information please e-mail the Special Markets Department at SPsales@harpercollins.com.

FIRST WILLIAM MORROW PAPERBACK EDITION PUBLISHED 2014.

Library of Congress Cataloging-in-Publication Data has been applied for.

ISBN 978-0-06-229347-3

14 15 16 17 18   DIX/RRD   10 9 8 7 6 5 4 3 2

To Christof

The Taste of Apple Seeds

La mémoire ne nous servirait à rien
si elle fût rigoureusement fidèle.

Memory would be of no use to us
if it were strictly truthful.

PAUL VALÉRY

Chapter I

GREAT-AUNT ANNA DIED FROM PNEUMONIA when she was sixteen. They couldn't cure it because her heart was broken and penicillin hadn't yet been invented. It happened late one July afternoon. Anna's younger sister, Bertha, ran howling into the garden and saw that with Anna's rattling, dying breath all the red currants in the garden had turned white. It was a large garden; the scores of old currant bushes groaned under the heavy weight of the fruit. They should have been picked long before, but when Anna fell ill nobody gave a thought to the berries. My grandmother often told me this story, because it was she who had discovered the currants in mourning. Since that time there had only ever been black currants and white currants in my grandmother's garden, and every attempt to plant a red bush had failed—only white berries would grow on the stems. But nobody minded: the white ones tasted almost as sweet as the red, when you juiced them they didn't ruin your apron, and the jelly they made had a mysteriously pale translucent shimmer. "Preserved tears," my grandmother called it. The shelves in her cellar still housed jars of all sizes with the currant jelly from 1981, a summer particularly rich in tears, Rosmarie's final one. Once when my mother was looking for some pickled cucumbers she came across a jar from 1945: the first postwar tears. She donated it to the windmill association, and when I asked her why on earth she was giving away Granny's wonderful jelly to a local museum she said that those tears were too bitter.

My grandmother Bertha Lünschen, née Deelwater, died long after Great-Aunt Anna, but for many years she hadn't known who her sister was, what her own name was, or whether it was winter or summer. She had forgotten what shoes, wool, or spoons were for. Over a decade she cast off her memories with the same fidgety ease with which she plucked at the short white locks of hair at the nape of her neck or swept invisible crumbs from the table. I had a clearer recollection of the noise the hard, dry skin of her hand made on the wooden kitchen table than of the features of her face. Also of the way her ringed fingers always closed tightly around the invisible crumbs, as if trying to catch the shadows of her spirit drifting by; but maybe Bertha just wanted to cover the floor with crumbs, or feed the sparrows that in early summer loved taking dust baths in the garden and were forever uprooting the radishes. The table she later had in the care home was plastic, and her hand fell silent.

Before her memory went completely, Bertha remembered us in her will. My mother, Christa, inherited the land, Aunt Inga the stocks and shares, Aunt Harriet the money. I, the final descendant, inherited the house. The jewelry and furniture, the linen and the silver were to be divided up between my mother and aunts. Bertha's will was as clear as springwater—and just as sobering. The stocks and shares were not particularly valuable, nobody except cows wanted to live on the pasture of the north German lowlands, there wasn't much money left, and the house was old.

Bertha must have remembered how much I used to love the house. But we didn't find out about her will until after the funeral. I went on my own; it was a long, circuitous trip involving a number of trains. I set off from Freiburg and had to travel the entire length of the country until finally, right up in the village of Bootshaven at the stop opposite my grandmother's house, I got off a bus. From a ghostly small-town station it had taken me around all the local villages until it was practically empty. I was worn down by the journey, the grieving, and the feelings of guilt you always have when someone dies whom you loved but didn't know very well.

Aunt Harriet had come, too. She wasn't called Harriet anymore; now her name was Mohani. But she wasn't wearing orange robes, nor was she bald. Only the wooden-bead necklace with a picture of her guru indicated her new state of enlightenment. And yet, with her short henna-red hair and Reebok trainers, she looked different from the other black-clad figures who were gathering in small groups outside the chapel. I was pleased to see Aunt Harriet again, although I felt uneasy and nervous when I realized that the last time I had seen her was thirteen years earlier. That was when we had had to bury Rosmarie, Harriet's daughter. The unease was a feeling I was very familiar with, because each time I looked at my face in a mirror I thought of Rosmarie. Her funeral had been unbearable; maybe it's always unbearable when fifteen-year-old girls are buried. As they told me afterward, I had fainted into a deep unconsciousness. All I could recall was that the white lilies on the coffin gave off a warm, damp, and sweet smell that stuck in my nostrils and fizzed in my throat. I couldn't breathe. Then I spun into a white hole.

I'd woken later, in the hospital. When I fell I had hit my head on a stone and the wound needed stitches. It left a scar above the bridge of my nose, a pale mark. That was the first time I had ever fainted, but since then I have fainted plenty of times. Fainting is a family trait.

After her daughter died, Aunt Harriet turned her back on her faith. She went to the Bhagwan—poor thing, her friends said. To the sect. Although they uttered the word "sect" in hushed tones, as if they feared that it was lying in wait, ready to pounce, shave their heads, and leave them to stagger through the streets of the world, clanging cymbals with childish delight, a clutch of abandoned lunatics like those from *One Flew Over the Cuckoo's Nest*. But Aunt Harriet didn't look as if she was planning to get out her cymbals at Bertha's funeral. When she saw me she gave me a hug and planted a kiss on my forehead. More precisely, without saying a word she kissed the scar on my forehead and then nudged me on to my mother, who was standing beside her.

My mother looked as if she had been crying for the past few days. When I saw her my heart tightened into a crinkled lump. How dreadful to have to bury your own mother, I thought as I put my arms around mine. My father was standing next to my mother, supporting her; he seemed much smaller than the last time I'd seen him and there were lines on his face I had never seen before. Aunt Inga stood to one side; she had come on her own. In spite of her red eyes she looked breathtaking. Her beautiful mouth arched downward, which on her face gave an impression of pride rather than sadness. And although her dress was modest and high-necked, it looked more like a little black number than a garment of mourning. She grasped both my hands, and I winced briefly when I got a small electric shock from her left hand. She was wearing her amber bracelet on her right wrist. Her hands felt warm, hard, and dry.

It was a sunny June afternoon. I looked around at the other people; there were flocks of white-haired women with thick-lensed glasses and black handbags. The ladies from Bertha's social circle. The former mayor had also turned up, and then of course there was Carsten Lexow—my mother's old teacher—as well as a few school friends, some distant cousins of my aunts and mother, and three tall men who stood beside one another seriously and awkwardly. They were immediately recognizable as former admirers of Aunt Inga's because they hardly dared look her in the eye but never let her out of their sight. The Koops—the neighbors—had come, and a few people I couldn't place, maybe from the care home, maybe from the funeral director's, maybe from Granddad's old law firm.

Afterward, everyone went to the café beside the cemetery to eat buttercake and drink coffee. As always happens after funerals, the mourners all started talking at once, first in a murmur, then gradually more loudly. The three admirers were now standing around Aunt Inga, their legs wide apart and their backs very straight. It seemed as if Aunt Inga had been expecting them to pay homage, but at the same time she accepted it with gentle irony.

The women from the social circle sat together and held a social. Grains of sugar and slivers of almonds stuck to their lips. They ate in the same way that they spoke: slowly, loudly, and constantly. My father and Herr Lexow helped the two waitresses, bringing silver platters heaped with square slices of buttercake from the kitchen and placing one coffee pot after another on the tables. The women from the social circle joked a little with these two attentive young gentlemen and tried to get them to join their group. While my father respectfully flirted back, Herr Lexow smiled anxiously and fled to the neighboring tables. He had to live here, after all.

When we left the café it was still warm. Herr Lexow fastened metal clips around the bottoms of his trouser legs and climbed onto a black bicycle that was leaning unlocked against a wall. He raised his hand briefly and rode off toward the cemetery. My parents and aunts stayed by the entrance to the café, squinting in the evening sun.

My father cleared his throat. "Those gentlemen from the law firm—you saw them. Bertha left a will."

So they *were* the lawyers. My father wasn't finished; he opened his mouth to speak again, but paused. The three sisters continued to look at the red sun and said nothing.

"They're waiting at the house."

It was summer when Rosmarie died, too, although in the evenings the scent of autumn had started to creep in from the meadows. You could cool down quickly by lying on the ground. I thought of my grandmother buried underground, of the damp black hole where she now lay. Peaty soil, black and rich, but beneath it, sand. The earth that had been shoveled into a heap beside her grave was drying out in the sun, and a constant trickle of sand was running off it, like an egg timer, into small moraines.

"That's me," Bertha had once groaned. "That's my head."

She nodded at the egg timer on the table and rose smartly from her chair. Her hip swiped the egg timer off the table. The thin wooden frame broke and the glass shattered, spattered. I was a child then and her illness had not yet reached the stage where it was particularly noticeable. I got down on my knees and spread the pale sand across the black-and-white stone floor with my index finger. The sand was very fine and twinkled in the light of the kitchen lamp. My grandmother stood beside me, sighing, and asked how I could have broken the lovely hourglass. When I said it was she who had done it she shook her head, over and over again. Then she swept up the grains of sand and the glass shards and tipped them into the dustbin.

*

Aunt Harriet took my arm, and I gave a start.

"Shall we go?" she asked.

"Sure."

I tried to free myself from her gentle grip; she let go straightaway. I could sense her giving me sideways glances.

We walked to the house; Bootshaven is a very small village. People nodded solemnly as we passed. Occasionally an old woman would stand in our way and offer her hand in condolence, although not to my father. I didn't know any of them, but they all seemed to know me and said softly—out of respect for our grief and yet with a barely suppressed triumph—that somebody had noticed I looked like the Christel lass. It took me a while to realize that the "lass" was my mother.

You could see the house from a fair distance. The façade was overrun with Virginia creeper, and the upstairs windows were nothing but rectangular recesses in the dark green undergrowth. The two old lime trees on the drive had grown as high as the roof. When I placed my hand on the wall of the house, the rough red stones felt warm. A gust of wind blew through the creeper, the limes nodded, the house gave a short sigh.

The lawyers were standing at the bottom of the steps that led up to the front door. One flicked away his cigarette when he saw us coming. Then he bent down swiftly to retrieve the butt. As we climbed the broad steps his head was bowed. He knew that we had seen him: the back of his neck had flushed red and he was rummaging around intently in his briefcase. The two other men were gazing at Aunt Inga; both of them were younger than her but they immediately started fawning over her. One of them took a key from his case and gave us an inquiring look. My mother took the key and slid it into the lock. When the brass bell by the topmost hinge of the door clanged noisily, the same half-smile appeared on the faces of all three sisters.

"Let's go into the study," Aunt Inga said, leading the way.

I was intoxicated by the aroma in the entrance hall: it still smelled of apples and old stone, and my great-grandmother Käthe's carved dower chest still stood by the wall. On either side of it were the oak chairs adorned with the family coat of arms: a heart divided by a saw. My mother's and Aunt Inga's heels clacked against the floor, sand crunched beneath leather soles; Aunt Harriet alone followed slowly and noise-lessly in her Reeboks.

Granddad's study had been tidied up. My parents and one of the lawyers, the young one with the cigarette, pushed four chairs together: three on one side and one opposite. The young lawyer then joined his colleague against the wall to the right. Unmoved by the commotion, Hinnerk's hefty desk remained by the wall between the two windows, which looked out onto the drive and the limes. The leaves refracted the sunlight, dappling the room; dust danced in the air. It was chilly in here. My mother and aunts sat on the three dark chairs, while the third lawyer took Hinnerk's desk chair. My father and I stood behind the three sisters. The legs and backs of the chairs were so tall and straight that the bodies sitting in them instantly snapped into right angles: feet and shins, thighs and back, upper arms and forearms, neck and shoulders, chin and neck. The sisters looked like Egyptian statues in a burial chamber. And although the flecked light dazzled us, it did not warm up the room.

The lawyer sitting on Hinnerk's desk chair fiddled with the locks on his briefcase; seeming to take this as a sign, the other two cleared their throats and looked seriously at him, obviously their boss. He introduced himself as the partner of the former partner of Heinrich Lünschen, my grandfather.

Bertha's will was read and explained, my father appointed executor. A ripple passed through the bodies of the sisters when they heard that the house had been left to me. I dropped down onto a stool and looked at the partner of the partner. I could see the lawyer with the cigarette staring at me, so I lowered my eyes and fixed them on the hymn sheet from the funeral service, which was still rolled up in my hand. The notes of "O Head Full of Blood and Wounds" had become imprinted on the heel of my palm. Inkjet printer. In my mind I saw heads full of blood and wounds, hair like jets of red ink, holes in heads, the gaps in Bertha's memory, sand from the egg timer. You could make glass from sand if it was hot enough. With my fingers I felt my scar: no, no sand was trickling out yet, only dust swirling from my skirt when I took my hand from my forehead and crossed my legs. I stared at a thin ladder that started at my knee then vanished beneath the black velvet of my skirt. I could sense Harriet's gaze, and looked up. Her eyes were full of pity; she hated the house. Rosemary, for remembrance. Who had said that? Forgotten.

The looser the mesh of Bertha's mind, the larger the chunks of memory that slipped through. As she became more confused, the woolen things she knitted became ever crazier: because she was constantly dropping stitches, knitting different patterns together, or starting new stitches at the seams, they grew and shrank in all directions, gaped and felted, and could be unpicked at any point. My mother had gathered together the pieces of knitting in Bootshaven and taken them back home. She had kept them in a box in her wardrobe. Once, by chance, I'd stumbled upon them; with a mixture of horror and amusement, I had laid out on my parents' bed one woolen sculpture after another. At that stage I wasn't living with my parents anymore and Bertha was already in the care home. My mother came in, and for a while both of us gazed at the woolen creatures.

"I suppose that each of us has to preserve our tears somewhere," my mother had said, as if defending herself, and then she packed everything away in the wardrobe. We never spoke about Bertha's knitting again.

We all walked out of the study in single file, back along the hallway and out the front door; the bell clanged tinnily. The lawyers offered us their hands then left, and we sat outside on the steps. Almost all the smooth yellow-white stones had cracks. Flat chunks of stone had come loose and you could lift them up like lids. In the past there hadn't been that many loose ones, only six or seven; we had used them as secret compartments, hiding feathers, flowers, and letters inside.

Back then I still wrote letters, I still believed in written, printed, and read matter. These days I no longer did. I had a job at the library at Freiburg University: I worked with books, I bought books, I even borrowed the odd one. But read them? No. I used to—oh yes, I used to read all the time, in bed, while eating, on my bike. But it stopped. Reading was the same as collecting, and collecting was the same as keeping, and keeping was the same as remembering, and remembering was the same as not knowing exactly, and not knowing exactly was the same as having forgotten, and having forgotten was the same as falling, and at some point you had to stop falling.

That was one explanation.

But I liked being a librarian. For the same reasons that I didn't read anymore.

I had started out studying German, but working on my essays I found that everything I did after compiling the bibliography seemed inconsequential. Catalogs, subject registers, reference books, indexes all had their own delicate beauty, which, if you gave them only a cursory reading, was as inaccessible as a hermetic poem. Whenever, starting with a general reference volume, its pages softened by the fingers of myriad readers, I gradually arrived via several other books at a highly specialized monograph whose cover nobody save for a librarian had touched before me, I felt a sense of satisfaction I could never gain from my own writing. And in any case, the things you wrote down were the things you didn't have to remember, that is to say the things you could safely forget because you knew where to find them, and thus what held true for reading applied to writing as well.

What I particularly loved about my job was rooting out forgotten books, books that had been sitting in the same spot for hundreds of years, probably never read, covered with a thick layer of dust, and yet which had outlived the millions of people who hadn't read them. I had already unearthed seven or eight of these books and would visit them occasionally, but I would never touch them. Sometimes I might breathe in their smell. Like most library books they had a stale odor, the very opposite of fresh. The book that smelled the worst was the one on ancient Egyptian friezes; it was terribly blackened and ragged.

I had visited my grandmother only once in the care home. She was sitting in her room, clearly frightened of me, and she wet herself. A nurse came and changed her nappy. I gave Bertha a good-bye kiss on the cheek; she was cold, and my lips felt the web of wrinkles that softly traversed her skin.

While I was waiting on the steps, tracing the cracks in the stone with my finger, my mother sat two steps higher, talking to me. She spoke quietly without finishing her sentences; her words seemed to hang in midair. Irritated, I wondered why she had started doing this of late. It was only when she put in my lap a large brass key—with the simple contour of its bit it looked like a stage prop for a fairy tale—that I finally grasped what was going on. It was all about the house: Bertha's daughters here on the weathered steps, her dead sister who had been born in the house, and Rosmarie who had died in the house. And it was all about the young lawyer with the cigarette. I had almost failed to recognize him, but he had to be the younger brother of Mira Ohmstedt, our best friend. Rosmarie's and my best friend.

Chapter II

MY PARENTS, MY AUNTS, AND I stayed the night in the three guest rooms at the village inn.

"We're going back down to Baden," my mother said the following morning. She said it a second time, as if needing to convince herself. Her sisters sighed; to them it sounded as if she were going back to happiness. And maybe that was the case. Aunt Inga would get a lift with them as far as Bremen. I gave her a quick hug and got an electric shock.

"This early in the morning?" I asked in astonishment.

"It's going to be hot today," Inga said apologetically. She crossed her arms over her chest and with a quick movement stroked from her shoulders down to her wrists. She then splayed her fingers and shook them. There was a slight crackle as sparks shot from her fingertips.

Rosmarie had loved the way Aunt Inga sparked. "Oh, please can we have some more shooting stars?" she would say, especially when we were out in the garden at night. Then we would watch in awe as for a split second tiny points of light danced on Aunt Inga's hands. "Doesn't that hurt?" we would ask, and she would shake her head. But I never believed her; she used to wince whenever she leaned against a car, opened a cupboard door, turned on a light or the television. Sometimes she dropped things. I would come into the kitchen and Aunt Inga would be crouched down, sweeping up shards with the hand brush. When I asked her what had happened, she would say, "Oh, just a silly accident—I'm so clumsy."

On those occasions when Inga couldn't avoid shaking hands with people she would apologize, as they often yelled in fright. Rosmarie called her "Sparky Fingers," but we all knew that she really admired Aunt Inga. "Why can't you do that, Mummy?" she asked Aunt Harriet once. "And why can't I?" Aunt Harriet had looked at her and said that it was the only way Inga could release her tension, and that Rosmarie was so energetic that she would never be capable of such discharges; it was something she should be thankful for.

Aunt Harriet had always been spiritual. She took a few inner journeys and wandered back again before she became Mohani and started wearing that wooden-bead necklace. As my mother saw it, when Harriet's daughter died she sought a father and became a daughter again herself. She wanted something solid. Something that would stop her from falling but also help her forget. I was never satisfied with this explanation: Aunt Harriet loved drama, not melodrama. She might be crazy, but she was never vulgar. She probably felt a connection with Osho, the dead guru. It must have been a comfort to her that a dead person could be so alive, because she had never seemed particularly impressed by the living Bhagwan, and she used to laugh at the pictures of him with his fleet of huge cars.

When my mother, father, and Aunt Inga had left, Aunt Harriet and I drank peppermint tea in the café. Our silence was wistful and relaxed.

"Are you going to the house now?" Aunt Harriet asked finally. She stood and picked up her leather travel bag, which was next to our table. Osho was smiling in the wooden-framed pendant of her necklace. I looked him in the eye and nodded. He nodded back. I stood up, too. She hugged me so tightly that it hurt. I said nothing and peered over her shoulder at the empty café. The haze of coffee and sweat, which yesterday had cloaked the funeral-goers in its warmth, still hung beneath the low white ceiling. Aunt Harriet kissed my forehead and left. Her Reeboks squeaked on the waxed floorboards.

On the street she turned and waved. I raised my hand. She turned back and stood at the bus stop. Her shoulders were hunched and her short red hair slipped beneath the collar of her black blouse. I was shocked. It was only from behind that I could see how unhappy she was. I looked away and sat back down at the breakfast table. I didn't want her to feel embarrassed. When the bus groaned as it left, rattling the windowpanes, I looked up and caught one last glimpse of Aunt Harriet; she was sitting, casting a frozen stare at the seat in front of her.

I walked back to the house. My bag wasn't heavy—there wasn't much in it besides the black velvet skirt—and I was wearing a short black sleeveless dress and black sandals with thick wedge heels: good for long distances on pavement or lugging books from shelves without twisting your ankle. There was little going on on that Saturday morning. A few teenagers were sitting on their mopeds outside the Edeka shop, eating ice cream. The girls were endlessly tossing their newly washed hair. It looked strange, as if their necks were too weak to support their heads, and I was afraid that at any moment their heads might snap backward or to the side. I must have been staring, because they all fell silent and returned my gaze. Although this was uncomfortable, I was relieved that the girls' heads had stopped wobbling and now sat upright on their necks rather than listing at strange angles on their shoulders or chests.

The main road curved sharply to the left; straight ahead a gravel road led past the BP petrol station and a couple of houses to the pastures. Later I wanted to pump up the tires on one of the bikes and cycle along this road to the lock. Or even to the lake. Aunt Inga had said it would get warm today.

I walked on the right-hand side of the road. To my left I could already see the large mill beyond the poplars. It had been freshly painted and I felt sorry for it, degraded by such color. After all, nobody would think of forcing the women of my grandmother's social circle to flounce around in glitzy leggings. Bertha's farmhouse, which was now to be my house, was opposite the mill. I stood at the bottom of the drive; the galvanized gate was locked but lower than I remembered, exactly at waist height, so I quickly straddled it and climbed over.

In the morning light the house was a dark, tatty box with a broad, ugly driveway. The lime trees were in the shade. On the way to the steps I saw that the entire front garden was overgrown with forget-me-nots. The blue flowers were just beginning to wither; some were fading, others were turning brown. A thicket of dying forget-me-nots. I bent down and pulled off a flower; it wasn't blue at all, it was gray and violet and white and pink and black. Who *had* been looking after the garden when Bertha was in the home? And what about the house? I planned to ask Mira's brother.

As I entered I was greeted once more by the aroma of apples and cold stone. I put my bag on the dowry chest and walked the length of the hallway. Yesterday we had only made it as far as the study. Today I didn't peek into any of the rooms but opened the door at the very end of the hall. To the right a steep staircase led upstairs, straight ahead there were two steps down, then the bathroom on the right, where my grandfather had come crashing through the ceiling one evening as my mother was washing me. Intent on giving us a fright, he had crept up to the attic above. The floorboards must have been rotten and my grandfather was a large, heavy man. He broke his arm and we weren't allowed to tell anybody what happened.

The door to the barn was locked. The key was hanging beside it on the wall, attached to a block of wood. I let it hang there. Then I climbed the stairs to the rooms where we used to sleep and play. The third step up creaked more loudly than before, but maybe the house had just got quieter. And the two at the top? Yes, they still creaked, and the third one from the top had joined them, too. The banisters whimpered the moment I touched them.

Upstairs the air was thick, old, and warm like the woolen blankets packed in the chests. I opened the windows on the large landing, the doors to the four main rooms, both doors of the walk-through room that had been my mother's, and finally the twelve windows in all five bedrooms. I didn't touch the skylight over the staircase; it was covered in a thick layer of cobwebs. Hundreds of spiders had spun their webs here over the years and the gossamer threads suspended not only dried-out flies but perhaps the dead bodies of their onetime owners as well. Matted together, the webs formed a soft white material, a milky light filter, rectangular and wan. I thought of the soft web of wrinkles on Bertha's cheeks; it was so wide meshed that daylight seemed to shimmer through her skin from behind. Bertha had become see-through with old age; her house was opaque.

"But both of them rather eccentric," I said out loud to the skylight, and the cobwebs fluttered in my breath.

Up here were the mighty old wardrobes. This was where we had played, Rosmarie, Mira, and I. Mira was a girl who lived nearby, she was a little older than Rosmarie and two years older than me. Everyone said that Mira was very quiet, though we didn't think so. She never said much but managed to breed disquiet wherever she went. I don't think it was just because of the black clothes she always wore—that was fairly common back then. Far more disquieting were her brown oval eyes: a white stripe divided the lower lids from her irises, and the black kohl line she drew only on her lower lids made her eyes look as if they were wrongly positioned on her face. Her upper lid hung down heavily, almost as far as the pupil. This gave her a slightly furtive but also languidly sensuous expression, for Mira was very beautiful. With her small mouth painted dark red, her dyed-black bob, those eyes and the eyeliner, she looked like a morphine-addicted silent movie star. When I last saw her she had just turned sixteen. Rosmarie would have also turned sixteen a few days later. I was fourteen.

Mira didn't just wear only black things, she ate only black things, too. In Bertha's garden she would pick blackberries, black currants, and only the darkest cherries. When the three of us went on a picnic we would always have to pack some bitter chocolate or black bread with black pudding. What was more, Mira only read books that she had wrapped in black paper beforehand, listened to black music, and washed with black soap that an aunt in England used to send her. In art lessons she would refuse to paint with watercolors, drawing only with Scribtol ink or charcoal, but she was better than everyone else, and as the art teacher had a soft spot for her she got away with it.

"It's bad enough that we have to paint on white paper, but bright colors, too!" she said scornfully, yet she liked drawing on white paper, you could see that.

"Do you also go to black masses?" Aunt Harriet had asked.

"They're not for me," Mira said casually, looking at my aunt from beneath those heavy eyelids. "I know everything's black, but I find it all too gross and loud." And she wasn't a Christian Democrat, either, she added with a wry smile. Aunt Harriet laughed and offered her the box of After Eights; Mira nodded and picked out a paper bag with the tips of her fingers.

Mira did have one passion, however. One that wasn't black. It was colorful and unpredictable and enigmatic—Rosmarie. Not even Aunt Harriet knew what became of Mira after Rosmarie died. All she knew was that she no longer lived in the village.

I kneeled on a dowry chest and leaned my arms on the windowsill. Outside, the leaves of the weeping willow were shimmering. The wind—I had almost forgotten it in the summer heat of Freiburg and behind the cool concrete walls of the university library. Wind was an enemy of books. In the special reading room for old and rare books it was forbidden to open the window. Ever. I tried to imagine what mischief the wind might get up to with the loose leaves of Jakob Böhme's three-hundred-and-seventy-year-old manuscript, *De signatura rerum*, and almost ended up closing the window again. There were many books up here. Some in each room, while the large landing served as storage space for all the things that weren't allowed into the cellar: anything made out of fabric, and books. I leaned farther out of the window and saw the climbing rose sprawling over the roof above the front door and tumbling from the railing past the little wall beside the steps.

My knees were hurting, so I slid down from the chest back into the room. Limping, I brushed along the bookshelves. Legal commentaries, their paper swollen and warped, were almost crushing the fragile *Nesthäkchen and the World War*; *Nesthäkchen*'s cracked spine had old German writing on it. I remembered that my grandmother's name was inside the book, in a child's Sütterlin script. The collected works of Wilhelm Busch propped itself peacefully up against Arthur Schnitzler's autobiography. Here was *The Odyssey*, there *Faust*. Kant snuggled up next to Chamisso, the collected letters of Frederick the Great stood back to back with *Pucki as a Young Housewife*. I tried to work out whether the books had been slotted into the shelves at random or ordered according to a particular system. Perhaps there was a code I had to recognize and decipher. They certainly hadn't been arranged by size. I could also rule out alphabetical or chronological order, as well as publisher, author's country of origin, or topic. Thus it had to be a random system. I didn't believe the books were put there randomly, but that there was a system that made it seem that way. And if there was a system to the randomness then it couldn't technically be random, which means a pattern could be figured out. Either that or it was all coincidental. The message of the books' spines was still hidden to me, but I resolved to keep it in the back of my mind. Over time something would click, I was sure of it.

How late was it? I never wore a watch; I relied on clocks at pharmacies, petrol stations, and jewelers' shops, station clocks and my relatives' alarm clocks. In the house there were a number of splendid clocks, but none of them worked. I was unsettled by the thought of being in this place without knowing the time. How long had I been staring at the books? Was it past lunchtime? The thicket of cobwebs in the skylight may have become even denser during the time that I had spent up here. I looked up at the shimmering rectangle and tried to compose myself by thinking in big units of time. Night hadn't passed yet, the funeral was yesterday, today was Saturday, tomorrow would be Sunday, I had taken off the day after that, then I would be going back down to Baden. But it didn't work. I cast a final glance at the bookshelves, closed all the windows, and went down the stairs, which continued to creak for a while even after I had reached the bottom.

Grabbing my rucksack, I lingered in the hallway. After being away for so long and now being alone in the house for the first time, I felt as if I was taking stock. What was still there, what wasn't, and what had I forgotten? What really had been different and what now felt different? Through the glass panes of the front door I could see the roses, the sun in the meadows and pasture. Where should I base myself? Upstairs was preferable; the rooms downstairs still belonged to my grandmother, even if she hadn't set foot in them over the past five years. She had been in the care home for almost thirteen years, but my aunts would often bring her back to the house for an afternoon. At some point, however, she didn't want to get into a car anymore, and later wasn't able to, couldn't walk, couldn't talk.

I opened the door to Bertha's bedroom. It was next to the study and its windows also looked out onto the drive with the limes. The venetian blinds were closed. Bertha's dressing table stood between the two windows. I sat on the stool, gazing into the large folding mirror, which looked like an open book. My hands reached for the two side panels and angled them slightly inward so that they were reflecting each other. As in the past, I could now see hundreds of images of my face. My scar shone white. I saw myself reflected so many times that I became disoriented. It was only when I folded one side panel flat again that I could work out where I was.

I went back upstairs and pushed the windows wide open once more. Up here were the old wardrobes with the once-beautiful garments made of soft, tired materials. As a child I had tried them all on. Over there were the old chests packed with ironed linen, nightshirts, and tablecloths bearing the monograms of my great-grandmother, Great-Aunt Anna, and Bertha, the pillows and sheets, woolen blankets, eiderdowns, crocheted covers, doilies, broderie anglaise, and substantial lengths of white curtains. The ceiling beams were bare, the doors gaped. And all of a sudden I felt a wrench, and then I couldn't help crying because everything was so terrible and so lovely at the same time.

I cried many other times, too.

I put my bag in my mother's old room, the walk-through room. I fished out my purse from a side pocket and raced down the stairs. If you ran they only squealed briefly. I took the key, which I'd hung on its hook, opened the front door—the bell clanged—and then I locked up behind me. Down the steps, a breath of roses in my lungs, a glance at the terrace—this was where the conservatory used to be— quickly, quickly through the rose arch and the garden gate, and I was out. There had to be a few things to eat at the petrol station just around the corner. I didn't fancy the Edeka shop and the teenagers' wobbling heads, nor being stared at out of curiosity—there were bound to be more people around now.

It was all happening at the petrol station. Here, the Saturday car wash was a ritual. Inside the shop, two boys were standing in front of the chocolate bars, their foreheads deeply furrowed. They didn't even look up when I squeezed past them. I bought some milk, black bread, cheese, a bottle of apple juice, and a large carton of multivitamin buttermilk, as well as a newspaper, a packet of crisps, and a bar of nut chocolate for an emergency. Well, two bars, just in case. I could always come back and get more if necessary. A dash to the till. As I left I saw the two boys in the same place, still deep in thought.

On Bertha's kitchen table my shopping looked out of place and rather silly: the bread in a plastic bag, the shrink-wrapped cheese, and the luridly colorful buttermilk carton. Maybe I should have gone to the Edeka shop after all. I picked up the cheese: six identical yellow squares. They were strange, these long-life things; perhaps the windmill association might even exhibit the cheese in their local museum someday. In the library I had once come across a book called *Eat Art*, which contained photos of food exhibited as artwork. The food itself was going bad but the photos had put a halt to the decay; the book was more than thirty years old. The food would have long since vanished, devoured by hungry bacteria, but on those yellowed glossy pages it was stranded in a sort of cultural limbo. There was something merciless about preserving; maybe the process of forgetting was in fact a dignified way of letting things go, rather than cruelly conserving them. All this thinking about food: I must be hungry. Maybe I ought to go back down to the cellar and look for the currant jelly. It tasted wonderful on black bread. I had forgotten to buy butter.

The kitchen was large and cold. The floor was made up of millions of tiny black and white square stones. I hadn't learned the word "terrazzo" until much later. As a child I could stare for hours at this stone pattern. At some point, when it started to swim before my eyes, secret symbols would suddenly appear on the kitchen floor. But they always vanished before I could decipher them.

There were three doors in the kitchen. I had entered from the hallway; another, bolted door led down to the cellar. The third door went out into the barn.

The barn was neither inside nor outside. Once a cowshed, it had a tamped-earth floor bordered by wide gutters. Three steps led down to it from the kitchen and at the bottom were the bins and a woodpile stacked up against the roughcast walls. If you went straight through the barn you came to another door, a green wooden door, and this really did lead outside, into the orchard. But if you turned right immediately, as I did now, you came to the utility rooms. The first door I opened was the one to the laundry, which had once housed a privy; now there were just two huge freezers. Both stood empty, their doors open, the plugs on the floor beside them.

From here a narrow staircase led up to the attic, from which my grandfather used to try to scare us. Behind the laundry was a room with an open fireplace. It used to be the anteroom to the conservatory, full of planters and jardinieres, watering cans and folding chairs. It had a light-colored stone floor and fairly new floor-to-ceiling glass sliding doors that led out onto the terrace. This had the same flagstones as inside. The branches of the weeping willow brushed against the flags and obscured the view to the exterior steps and the front door.

I sat on the sofa beside the black fireplace and gazed out. There was no longer any sign of the conservatory; it had been an elegant construction that must have clashed with the solid brick house. Just glass and a steel frame. Aunt Harriet had had it dismantled thirteen years earlier. After Rosmarie's accident. The flagstones, which were actually too delicate for the outside, reminded me of the glass structure.

I suddenly realized that I didn't want it, this house. It had stopped being a house a long time ago; it was now only a memory, just like the conservatory that didn't exist anymore. When I got up to push open the sliding doors I felt how clammy my hands were. Outside it smelled of moss and shadows. I pushed the doors closed again. The burned-out fireplace radiated the cold. I would tell Mira's brother that I didn't want my inheritance. But right now I had to get out of here, get out and go to the lock by the river. I dashed back into the barn and searched through the clutter for a bicycle that might work. All the newer ones were in bad shape, but Granddad's very old, gearless black bike just needed the tires pumping up.

I couldn't leave without taking a long and convoluted tour of the house, to bolt some doors from the inside, then going out through other doors that had to be locked from the outside, and so I finally ended up in the garden. For quite a long time Bertha had retained the ability to find her way around the house. At the point when she wasn't able to go to the mill without getting lost she could still get straight from the laundry to the bathroom, even if one or another door on the way was locked on the other side. Over the decades she had so fused with the house that, had they performed an autopsy on her, I'm sure by looking at the twists and turns in her brain or the network of her veins they would have been able to produce a route map of the house. With the kitchen at its heart.

I had put the food from the petrol station into a basket that I found on top of a kitchen cupboard. The handle was broken, so I fastened it to the pannier rack and wheeled the bike out of the barn through the door that led into the garden. Everyone called this the kitchen door, even though it didn't lead out of the kitchen but could only be seen from it. The willow branches brushed against my head and the handlebars. I pushed the bike past the steps, then to the right along the house, ankle-deep in forget-me-nots. On one of the hooks by the front door I had found a flat stainless-steel key, and because the only new door was the galvanized gate at the end of the drive, I tried it out. The key turned willingly and then I was standing on the pavement.

After passing the petrol station I veered left onto the pathway to the lock; on Hinnerk's heavy bike I almost skidded on some sand in the bend, but recovered at the last moment and started pedaling more firmly. The springs beneath the leather saddle squeaked cheerfully as the asphalt gradually became riddled with potholes and soon turned into a gravel farm track. I knew this path, which went in a straight line through the cow pasture. I knew the birch trees, the telegraph poles, the fences—no, lots of them must be new, obviously. I also thought I recognized the black pied cows, but that was complete nonsense, of course. As I cycled, the wind buffeted my dress; although it was sleeveless, I still felt hot as the dark material absorbed the sun's heat. For the first time since I had arrived I felt I could breathe again.

The path continued straight ahead, sometimes dipping a little, sometimes rising; I closed my eyes. They had all been down this path. Anna and Bertha riding in a carriage, wearing white muslin dresses. My mother, Aunt Inga, and Aunt Harriet on Rixe ladies' bikes. And Rosmarie, Mira, and me on the same Rixe bikes, which rattled dreadfully and whose saddles were too high, which meant that most of the time we had to cycle in a standing position to avoid dislocating our hips. But we would not have lowered the saddles for anything: it was a matter of honor. We used to cycle in old dresses belonging to Anna, Bertha, Christa, Inga, and Harriet. The headwind would billow the light blue tulle and the black organza, and the sun reflected in the golden satin. We would fasten up our clothes with pegs so that they didn't get caught up in the chains. And we would cycle barefoot to the river.

You were not supposed to ride for too long with your eyes closed, not even in a straight line. I almost scraped a cow fence; it wasn't much farther now. In the distance I could already see the wooden bridge over the lock. On the bridge I stopped, holding on tightly to the railings without taking my feet off the pedals. No one there. Two sailing boats were moored to the jetty, metal clanking quietly against the masts.

I got off, wheeled the bike from the bridge, unclipped the basket, left the bike on the grass, and walked down the slope. The ground didn't fall away steeply to the water; instead it formed a gentle bank, overgrown with reeds. We used to spread out our towels where we could, but over the years it had become so overgrown that I now chose to sit on one of the wooden jetties.

My feet were dangling in blackish-brown water. Bog water. How white they looked, and unfamiliar. To distract myself from the sight of my feet I tried to read the names of the boats. One of them was called "Syne," but that was just a part of it, a wreck of a name. I couldn't make out the name of the second one; it was facing the other side of the river. Something with "-the" at the end. I lay on my back and left my unfamiliar feet where they were; the lock smelled of water, meadow, mustiness, and wood preservative.

How long had I slept? Ten minutes? Ten seconds? I was freezing. I took my feet out of the water and reached above my head for the basket. What my fingers touched wasn't brittle wickerwork but a trainer. I wanted to scream, but all that came out was a groan. I rolled straight onto my stomach and pushed myself up. Silver dots were floating before my eyes and there was a whooshing in my head, as if the lock gate beside me had just opened. The sun glinted, the sky was white, white. Don't faint now, I told myself; it was a narrow jetty, I would drown.

"Oh my God, I'm so sorry. Please excuse me, please."

I knew that voice. The whooshing got quieter. In front of me stood the young lawyer in his tennis gear; I was so angry

I could have been sick. Mira's dim-witted younger brother, what was it they used to call him?

"Oh, it's the Wimp!" I tried to sound calm.

"I know, I frightened you and I'm really sorry." His voice became steadier and I could hear a spark of irritation in it. That was fine. I looked at him and said nothing. "I didn't follow you or anything like that—I always come here to swim. First I play tennis, you see, and then I go for a swim; my partner never comes, but I'm always here on the jetty; I didn't see you until I got down here and then I saw you were sleeping and was about to go again, but you grabbed my trainer—of course you didn't know it was my trainer, but even if you had I wouldn't have held it against you because, after all, it was me who frightened you, and now . . ."

"My God, do you always go on like that? Even in the courtroom? Have you really got a permanent job with that law firm?"

Mira's brother laughed. "Iris Berger. I was only ever the Wimp to you lot, and it doesn't look as if that's ever going to change."

"I suppose not."

I bent down and reached for my basket. Even though Mira's brother had a nice laugh I was still furious. I was also hungry, and I wanted to be alone and not have to talk. And no doubt he wanted to talk about the will, what I was planning to do with the house, and tell me that I should have it insured and about everything in store for me when the will came through. But I didn't want to talk about it now, didn't even want to think about it.

When I stood up again, basket in hand and mentally

composed to give my great speech, I was surprised to see that Mira's brother had already trudged halfway up the embankment. He trod heavily up the slope. I smiled.

There were patches of red sand on the right shoulder of his white T-shirt.

After the picnic I tidied everything away into the basket, took a final glance at the river, the lock, the boats; the second one had moved a little, but I still couldn't make out the whole name—something ending in "-ethe," Margarethe maybe, that was a good name for a boat. I climbed onto Hinnerk's bike and rode back to the house. To *my* house. How did that sound? Weird, and fake somehow. The wind blew snatches of a chiming bell across the pasture but I couldn't hear how late it was. It felt like early afternoon, one or two o'clock, maybe later. The sun, food, anger and fright, and now the head-on wind made me tired. After the petrol station I turned onto the pavement, then dismounted on the drive. I hadn't locked the gate, and I waded through the forget-me-nots and leaned the bike by the kitchen door. I let myself in with the large key. A brass clanking, another brass clanking, and then I was in the cool hallway. The stairs groaned, the banisters moaned, it was hot and sticky below the roof. I threw myself onto my mother's bed; why had it been freshly made? A purple pillow twinkled beneath the broderie anglaise. The holes were flowers. Holes in the pillow. The point of broderie anglaise was what wasn't there. That was the art of it. If there were too many holes, there would be nothing left. Holes in the pillow, holes in the head.

*

When I woke up, my tongue was stuck to the roof of my mouth. I staggered through the left-hand door into Aunt Inga's room, which had a washbasin; brackish brown water spluttered petulantly into the white sink. In the mirror I looked at the pattern the pillow cover had made on my cheek: red rings. Gradually the water flowed more evenly, slowly getting clearer. I splashed water onto my face, took off my sweaty clothes—dress, bra, knickers, everything— and enjoyed standing there naked in Aunt Inga's room, the gray-green lino cold beneath my toes. Aunt Inga had been the only one not to have carpet in her room; my mother, Great-Grandma Käthe, and Aunt Harriet, who were at the back of the house, had a hard, rust-colored sisal carpet that scratched the soles of your feet if you walked across it barefoot. On the large landing there were raffia mats on the wood. It was only the girls' room, which had long been a storage room, that had bare floorboards, but these were coated in a thick brown varnish. They no longer made a sound.

I went onto the landing, opened the walnut wardrobe, and found that all the dresses were still hanging there; a little less vibrant but there, unmistakably, was the tulle dream from Aunt Harriet's end-of-dancing-course ball, the golden dress my mother had worn to her engagement party, and that black spangly-sparkly number, a tea gown from the thirties. It was one of Bertha's. I rummaged further until I came across an ankle-length green silk dress, the top half of which was embroidered with sequins. It belonged to Aunt Inga. I put it on; it smelled of dust and lavender, the hem was torn and there were some sequins missing, but it was cool against my body and felt a thousand times better than my black one that I had slept in. I had never before spent so long in the house without swapping my outfit for one from the old wardrobes; in my own clothes I felt as if I had been in disguise all day long.

Wearing Inga's silk dress I went back into her room and sat on the wicker chair. The afternoon sun that flickered through the treetops bathed the room in a lime-green light. The streaks in the lino seemed to move like water, a breeze came in through the open window, and it felt as if I were sitting in the tranquil current of a green river.

Chapter III

AUNT INGA WORE AMBER. Long chains of polished beads in which you could see tiny insects. We were convinced that they would shake their wings and fly away the second their resinous shells broke. Around Inga's wrist was a chunky milky-yellow bracelet. She didn't wear this jewelry from the sea because of her deep-sea bedroom and mermaid dress, but, as she said, for health reasons. Even as a baby she gave everyone who held her an electric shock, barely noticeable, but the spark was there; and at nighttime when Bertha put her on her breast she got a sharp shock from her child, almost like a bite, before Inga started suckling. Bertha didn't talk to anybody about it, not even to Christa, my mother, who was two at the time and who used to flinch whenever she touched her sister.

The older Inga got, the stronger her electrical charge became. Soon other people noticed it, too, but then every child has something that marks them out from others and that people either tease them for or admire. In Inga's case it was these electric shocks. Hinnerk, my grandfather, got angry when Inga was close to the radio and upset the reception. There would be static, and through the hissing and crackling Inga would sometimes hear voices talking softly to one another or calling her name. As a result, when Hinnerk was listening to the radio she wasn't allowed into the living room. Mind you, he always listened to the radio when he was in the living room. When he wasn't in the living room he sat in the study, where no one was allowed to disturb him anyway. This meant that during the colder months of the year Hinnerk and Inga saw each other only at mealtimes. In summer everyone was outside, and in the evenings Hinnerk would sit on the terrace or ride his bike through the pasture. Inga avoided riding a bike: too much metal, too much friction. It was more Christa's thing, and so on summer evenings and Sundays Christa and Hinnerk would ride to the lock, the lake, and to cousins in the neighboring villages. Inga stayed close to home; she rarely left the property and thus knew it better than the rest of us.

Frau Koop, Bertha's neighbor, used to tell us girls that Inga was born during a violent storm; lightning had been raging overhead, and at the very instant that a bolt had flashed through the house from top to bottom, Inga was born. Inga hadn't made a sound; the first cry came from her mouth when the thunder boomed, and from then on she was electric. "The littl 'un," Frau Koop would tell anyone willing to listen, "hadn't been earthed yet," but was still "half hanging in the other world, the poor little worm." Admittedly, Rosmarie had come up with "the poor little worm" afterward. But if Frau Koop hadn't actually said that, it was definitely what she meant. In any case, we would never tell each other this story without adding the "poor little worm" at the end; we thought it sounded so much better like that.

Christa, my mother, had inherited the height and the long, rather pointy nose of the Deelwaters. From the Lünschens she had her thick brown hair, but her lips were sharply defined, her eyebrows strong, and her gray eyes narrow. Too severe to be considered a beauty in the fifties. I looked like my mother, only everything about me, my head, my hands, my body, even my knees, was rounder than Christa. Too round to be considered a beauty in the nineties. So that was another thing we had in common. Harriet, the youngest, wasn't exactly pretty, but looked lovely—always a little disheveled, with red cheeks, chestnut-brown hair, and healthy teeth that were slightly crooked. Her loping stride and large hands were reminiscent of a puppy. But Inga, she was beautiful. As tall as Bertha, if not taller, with a grace in the way she moved and a sweetness in her features that somehow refused to fit into the barren landscape here. Her hair was dark, darker than Hinnerk's, her eyes were blue like her mother's but larger and framed by curled dark eyelashes. Her red lips curved mockingly. She spoke in a soft, clear voice, though her vowels resonated deeply, which filled even the most empty words with promise. All men fell in love with Inga. But my aunt always kept them at arm's length; this wasn't so much coyness on her part as fear of the physical repercussions if she kissed them, let alone made love to them. So she withdrew, stayed at home listening to music on a bulky record player that a smart admirer who was good with his hands had made for her out of spare parts, and danced alone on the matte lino floor of her bedroom.

Besides a few electronics textbooks, her bookshelves contained fat, sad romance novels. My mother told us that when they were young the thing Inga enjoyed reading most of all was one particular story in the tattered old book of fairy tales that had belonged to my great-grandmother Käthe: the tale of the Amber Witch. Maybe Inga thought she was an amber witch herself, living at the bottom of the sea, luring people into the depths. She had started wearing amber jewelry as a child, because in one of the electronics textbooks she had read that *elektron* was the Greek word for amber, a substance particularly good at absorbing electric charges.

After finishing school she did a photography apprenticeship and now had her own highly regarded studio in Bremen. She specialized in photographing trees and plants, held small exhibitions from time to time, and received ever larger commissions for waiting rooms, conference halls, and other spaces where people stared at walls for hours on end and discovered for the first time that tree trunks could be as smooth as a woman's legs in silk stockings, that the fruits of the cranesbill really did look like cranes' bills, and that most old trees had human features. Inga never married. She was now in her midfifties and more beautiful than most women of twenty-five.

Rosmarie, Mira, and I were convinced that she had lovers. Aunt Harriet had once hinted that the DIY friend who made the record player had revealed his feelings for Inga, but she was still living at home at the time: for the three sisters, love affairs under Hinnerk's gaze were out of the question.

Rosmarie used to wonder what happened to our aunt's lovers. Did they die from heart failure just as they reached the most satisfying and blissful moment of their lives? What a glorious death, Rosmarie thought. Mira said that maybe Inga avoided all skin contact by doing everything in a wafer-thin rubber suit. "A black one, of course," she added.

I said that she probably did it like everyone else, only she might have to be earthed to a radiator or something similar beforehand.

"Do you think it hurts her?" Mira wondered.

"Shall we ask?"

But not even Rosmarie dared do that.

Inga photographed people, too, but only family members. More precisely, she only ever photographed her mother. The more Bertha's personality faded, the more obsessively Inga took portraits of her. In the end she only took photographs with a flash, partly because my grandmother hardly ever left her room in the care home—by then she had forgotten how to walk—but also because, however irrational she knew it was, Inga hoped that the flash would help her cut through the fog that was settling ever more thickly on Bertha's brain.

After my visit to Bertha four years earlier, Aunt Inga had showed me a whole crate of black-and-white photos of her mother. In the last four films Bertha always wore the same expression of uncomprehending horror, her mouth slightly open and her eyes wide, pinpricked with tiny pupils that had contracted instinctively. But there was no sign of awareness or discomfort. Bertha no longer knew anything nor wanted anything. The photos were well thumbed. Some were out of focus or blurred; that wasn't like Aunt Inga. The blaze of the camera flash had burned off the deep wrinkles on Bertha's face so that it stood out smooth and white against the hazy gray background. As white as the plastic table she wiped with her hand, and just as empty.

After I had given the photos back to Aunt Inga she gave her pictures another good look before putting them back in the crate. It was plain that Inga knew each individual picture in great detail and was able to distinguish them all from one another, because when she sorted them she seemed compelled to put them in a specific order. I wanted to put my arm around my aunt, but that was not so easily done, so I squeezed her hand tight in both of mine. She was totally absorbed with ordering her grotesque, identical portraits, and all the while her amber bracelet knocked against the crate with a clunk.

The metallic creak of a kickstand in the yard below and then the snap of a pannier rack sounded through the open window. I leaned out, but the visitor had already gone around the corner to ring at the front door. I thought I recognized the bicycle. The doorbell chimed, a real bell with a clapper. I dashed down the stairs, ran along the corridor, and tried to spy who it was through the glass panes. It was an old man; he was standing by the window so I could see who he was.

Surprised, I opened the door. "Herr Lexow!"

The friendly smile he had intended to greet me with gave way to an expression of uncertainty when he saw me. I remembered what I was wearing and felt embarrassed. He must have thought I was some kind of morbid lunatic, rummaging naked through the wardrobes upstairs and dancing wildly in bizarre costumes across the landing or even on the roof; after all, some family members had been known to do this in the past.

"Oh, please excuse my outfit, Herr Lexow." I was stammering as I struggled to find an explanation. "I-I'm afraid my dress had a terrible stain on it and as I've hardly got any spare clothes—it's so sticky in the house, you see . . ."

His friendly smile had quickly returned. He raised his hand sympathetically. "That's your aunt Inga's dress, isn't it? It looks fantastic on you. The thing is, I thought that someone might want to stay in the house. And as there's practically nothing in the kitchen I thought—I took the liberty—well, I simply wanted . . ."

Now it was Herr Lexow who was stammering. I took a step backward to let him in, closed the front door, and took the cotton bag that he had been holding out to me while he spoke. Before I could think about which room to show him into, he asked permission to go ahead and walked along the hallway to the kitchen. There he gently took the bag back from me, fished out a large tupperware bowl, opened one of the lower cupboards without much deliberation, grabbed a saucepan and put it on the cooker. I moved a few steps closer. He didn't say anything more, but moved around Bertha's kitchen with calm familiarity. Now I no longer needed to ask Mira's brother who had been looking after the house and garden in Bertha's absence. I shifted my weight from one foot to the other indecisively. Although the kitchen was large I was getting in the way.

"Would you mind fetching some parsley from the garden, my dear child?" Herr Lexow passed me some scissors.

From the yard the path led between the two lime trees into Bertha's kitchen garden. Italian honeysuckle rambled over the fence; the garden gate was ajar and it squeaked when I pushed it. There was parsley right at the front, overgrown with nasturtiums—"capers," as Bertha and her daughters used to call them. In late summer my mother always kept in the fridge a small jar of the bright green fruits from these flowers, but I didn't recall them ever being used in any cooking. What was this thin row of parsley doing growing here, anyway? Someone must have sown it. The same went for the unkempt pea and bean plants that were blossoming white and pink and orange. Here was a crooked row of leeks. On the ground, hairy cucumber vines were crawling between couch grass and camomile, trying to cast aside the weeds with their gray leaves, or at least infect them with blight.

Lemon balm and mint had taken over the beds and were running riot between the white currants, the ailing gooseberry bushes, and the blackberry canes, which were escaping over the fence into the neighboring copse. Herr Lexow must have tried to maintain Bertha's kitchen garden, but he didn't have her talent for allotting every plant its rightful space and gently coercing the best out of it.

I walked through the kitchen garden to take a look at Bertha's old perennials, which either honored my grandmother's memory or defied its disintegration—it amounted to the same thing. The billowing thicket of phlox had a delicate fragrance. Delphiniums thrust blue spikes into the evening sky. Lupins and marigolds shone above the soil, bellflowers nodded at me. The plump, heart-shaped hosta leaves barely left a patch of earth visible; behind these, hydrangeas, a whole hedge full, frothed bluish-pink and pinkish-blue from their foliage. Dark yellow and rosy parasols of yarrow swayed over the paths, and when I'd pushed them back my hands smelled of herbs and summer holidays.

Between the currants and the brambles was the wilder part of the garden. But now it had hidden itself in its own shadows. Behind the garden the pine copse began. Here the ground was rust red and consisted entirely of fallen needles. With every step you sank before springing back up, softly and silently, and you walked through as if spellbound until reaching the large orchard on the other side. In the past, Rosmarie, Mira, and I had hung old net curtains between the trees and built fairy houses in which we acted out long, complicated romantic dramas. To begin with these were just tales of three princesses who had been abducted and sold by a disloyal chamberlain, managed to escape from their ghastly foster parents after years of servitude, and now were living in the forest where, by happy coincidence, they were reunited with their real parents. After that the princesses went back and punished all those who'd ever done them an injustice. Rosmarie performed the "escape," I did the "reunion" and Mira the "revenge."

I went to the gate that led to the copse and peered into the dark green. I was met with a resinous and chilly greeting. I froze, gripped the scissors more firmly, and returned to the parsley. No sooner had I cut a large bunch than I caught its smell of earth and cooking, even though the herb's leaves were yellowing. Should I cut a bunch of lovage, too? Best not. I thought of that long-ago afternoon in the garden with Rosmarie and Mira. That was the last time I had spoken to Mira.

I straightened, walked through the barn door—the tamped-earth floor was ice-cold—bolted the door behind me, lifting the iron bars onto their hook, ran up the steps to the kitchen and almost became giddy at the smell of vegetable soup wafting through the room. I placed the bundle of parsley beside the steaming pan. Herr Lexow thanked me and glanced up. I had been away a long time for such a short errand.

"Almost there. I've set the table here in the kitchen."

And indeed, there was a white bowl on the kitchen table, and next to it a large silver spoon.

"But you've got to have some, too! Please, Herr Lexow."

"All right then, dear Iris. I'd love to."

We sat at the table, the pan of soup in front of us, the finely chopped parsley on a board beside it. We ate the wonderful broth, which was swimming with thick pieces of carrot and chunks of potato, peas, diced green beans, and a huge number of translucent leek rings. Herr Lexow fidgeted. He wanted to say something but I didn't realize this until I looked up to say something myself.

"HerrLexowdearIris," we began together.

"You first," I said.

"No, please, you."

"Okay. I just wanted to thank you for this soup at just the right time—what must the time be now? Also for having kept an eye on the house and looking after the garden. Thank you so much. I don't know how we can ever repay you, all the time and . . . love you've put in here, and . . ."

Herr Lexow interrupted me. "Stop. I want to tell you something, something that not many people know. To be precise, there are only two of us now; we buried the third yesterday, and I wonder if even she remembered. Now look, seeing as you were talking of love, well, when you opened the door wearing this dress, I—"

"I'm sorry, I can see just how tasteless it must have seemed to you, but I—"

"No, no, no. When you opened the door, I thought . . . You see, your aunt Inga—well, Inga and I . . ."

"You're in love with her? She's gorgeous."

Herr Lexow frowned. "Yes. No, not what you're thinking, maybe. I love her as a, as a . . . father."

"Yes, of course. I understand."

"No, I can see that you don't. I love her as a father because that's what I am."

"A father."

"Yes. No. *Her* father. *I'm* Inga's father. I loved Bertha. Always, to the very end. For me it was an honor, an obligation, a duty to keep an eye on her house. Please, don't thank me, I find it embarrassing, it was the very least I could do for her, I mean, after all . . ."

Beads of sweat were appearing on Herr Lexow's forehead. He was almost in tears. I had stopped eating. Inga's father. I hadn't expected that. But actually, why not? Did Inga know?

"Inga does know, I wrote to tell her when Bertha went into the home. I offered to check that everything was in order until . . . well, for as long as Bertha stayed there." Herr Lexow recovered his composure, his voice becoming steadier.

I got up, went into my grandparents' bedroom, and fetched myself a pair of Hinnerk's woolen socks and a gray-brown cardigan of Bertha's from the oak wardrobe. I sat on the stool by the dressing table to put the socks on. Bertha an adulteress? I staggered back into the kitchen. The soup had been cleared away and two mugs were on the table. Herr Lexow—my aunt's father, so my great-uncle of sorts—was stirring something in a small pan on the cooker. I sat on my chair and drew my feet onto the seat under me. Shortly afterward, milk was steaming in the mugs. Herr Lexow sat back down and told me, in a few words, what had happened.

Chapter IV

CARSTEN LEXOW ARRIVED IN BOOTSHAVEN as a young teacher. He was only twenty and came from Geeste, a village near Bremen. The school in Bootshaven had one large classroom in which all children of school age were lumped together. A single teacher taught everything and to everyone at the same time. Just once a year, a week after the end of the summer holidays, the pastor turned up and greeted the new confirmands.

Carsten's father had been a haberdasher and had died of a war injury four years before his son moved to Bootshaven. A French rifle bullet had roamed around his body for almost eight years before one day finally ending its wanderings in his lung and thus also ending the life of the haberdasher Carsten Lexow Senior. Carsten's father was a taciturn man who spent so much time in his shop that he forever remained a stranger to the family. Carsten's mother blamed this on the roaming bullet, which had stopped him from ever really coming home, but maybe it was just his manner. Much about him was short, not only the needles and pins he sold, but also his legs, his nose, and his hair, as well as his sentences and his temper. The only thing that was long was the path that the rifle bullet had traveled in his squat body, but when it finally reached its goal his death—just like his life—was short.

Widow Lexow continued to run the haberdashery on her own; Carsten sometimes helped out with the books. He had no siblings, but his mother's younger brother, a high-ranking official with the postal service and a bachelor, offered to lend his sister and nephew a hand. As Carsten showed no particular inclination to sell sewing thread and hat elastic, the widow agreed to send her son to Bremen for teacher training. Carsten spent two years there before he got the post in Bootshaven without even having applied for the job.

The old teacher had died of a heart attack, right in the middle of a lesson, but as he had a habit of nodding off in class none of the children had paid any attention to the hunched figure. As they always did when he fell asleep, the fourteen children left the room quietly giggling when the afternoon bell rang. Also as usual, they forgot the teacher until they saw him still asleep at his desk in exactly the same position the following morning. Nobody was surprised that the school and the classroom were unlocked; the old teacher had always been absentminded. But finally the eldest pupil, Nikolaus Koop, plucked up his courage and spoke to the small pale man, whose head had slumped so far onto his chest that only the crown was visible. When he didn't answer, Nikolaus took a step closer and had a good look at his teacher.

Like almost all the people in the village, the Koops were farmers. Nikolaus had often helped out with the slaughtering and had once seen a cow die while giving birth. He blinked a few times, turned to the other children, and said calmly, with long pauses between the words, that there wouldn't be any school today, they should all go home. Although Nikolaus was a shy boy who was often the first one out when they played dodgeball, and although he wasn't the class leader in spite of being the eldest, all the pupils left obediently. Anna Deelwater and her younger sister, Bertha, left the school-house with the other children. Their farmhouse was next to Nikolaus's and the three of them always walked to and from school together. On this day, however, the sisters went home without him, silently, their heads bowed.

Nikolaus Koop rang the bell of the parsonage, which was next to the school, and told the pastor what had happened. The pastor had been sitting at his desk, leafing through the paper. That same day the pastor wrote to his friend the pastor of Geeste, and three days later Carsten Lexow came to Bootshaven as the village teacher, just in time for the funeral of his predecessor. It was a blessing for everyone. The villagers were delighted to get a close look at the new teacher so soon. And Carsten Lexow counted himself lucky that he was wearing the black suit that he had had made for his father's funeral. It was also a good opportunity to introduce himself to everybody before they started making up stories about him. Of course they made up stories anyway, for Carsten Lexow was tall and slim with dark hair that he had difficulty keeping to one side, only managing it with a severe parting. His eyes were blue, but one day in class Anna Deelwater discovered, as he looked up from her exercise book, which he had been marking, that his pupils were hemmed with golden rings, and from that moment to the end of her life, which was not a long time, she remained chained to these rings.

There was only a single photograph of Anna Deelwater, the eldest daughter of Käthe, actually Katharina, and Carl Deelwater, but many copies of it. My mother had one, there was one hanging in Aunt Inga's house, and Rosmarie had stuck one in her wardrobe with tape. Aunt Anna—that was what my aunts and my mother called her when they spoke about her—Aunt Anna was dark-haired like her mother. In the photo it looked as if she had dark eyes, too, but Aunt Inga maintained that this was because of the poor lighting. What could be said with certainty was that she had drawn-out gray eyes and broad eyebrows that formed crescents rather than a straight line. Anna's eyebrows dominated her face, giving it something secretive and wild at the same time. She was shorter than her sister, but not as thin. Although Bertha, long-legged, fair, and cheerful, seemed to be the very opposite of her sister in appearance and character, both girls in fact were reserved, almost shy, and absolutely inseparable. They would whisper and giggle just as much as other girls of their age, but only ever together. Some people thought they were haughty, because Carl Deelwater owned the most pastureland and the biggest farmhouse in Bootshaven. He had also bought a pew for himself and his family in the front row of the church, engraved with his surname. Not that he was particularly religious. He seldom went to church, but when he did, on the high festivals such as Easter, Christmas, and Harvest Festival, he sat at the front in his own pew with his wife and daughters, and was gawked at by the other members of the small parish. On the many Sundays in the year when he didn't go to church, the pew remained empty and was gawked at all the same. Anna and Bertha were proud of their beautiful farmhouse and their wonderful father who, although he worried about who would succeed him at the farm, never held it against his daughters or his wife but sought to spoil his "three lasses" as much as possible.

Both daughters had to pitch in at home; they lent a hand to their mother in the house and helped Agnes, the maid, in the kitchen. Agnes came every day and was not a maid at all but a grown woman with three adult sons. With Agnes they made juice and plucked chickens. But what they enjoyed most of all, and spent most time doing, was working outside in the garden.

From the end of August they were rarely out of the apple trees. The light bell-shaped apples were ready first; they tasted of lemon, and from the moment you took your first bite it was impossible to finish them before the flesh started turning brown. These were never cooked to a pulp; their aroma vanished like the August wind they had ripened in. Then, slowly, came the apples on the Cox's Orange trees; the big one first of all, which grew very close to the house and basked in the heat given off by the red clinker bricks that had stored up the sun throughout the day. This meant that its fruit was always larger and sweeter than that of the other apple trees.

By October, all the trees had fruited. Anna and Bertha moved almost as nimbly in the trees as on the ground. Some years before, a gardener had nailed a few boards to the branches of a particularly heavily laden Boskoop tree so that they could sit their baskets on them. But the girls preferred sitting there themselves. They would read books to each other, drink juice, and eat apples and sometimes buttercake, which Agnes always brought out to them when one of her sons had stopped by. At least this meant she could say, if anyone ever asked why only one of the two tins of buttercake was left, that Bertha and Anna had eaten some, too. But nobody ever did ask.

Of course, Herr Lexow didn't tell me about Agnes's buttercake. I don't think he even knew that Agnes existed. I was sitting at the kitchen table in Bertha's house, seeing my grandmother and great-aunt as children, although in my mind Anna never looked any different from how she did in the photograph. Sipping a mug of lukewarm UHT milk I recalled things Bertha had told my mother and my mother had told me, or that Aunt Harriet had told Rosmarie and Rosmarie had told Mira and me, and things we had made up or at least imagined. On occasion Frau Koop had told us how when he was a boy her husband had found his teacher dead in the classroom. Nikolaus Koop had become a good-natured, hardworking farmer who had a cataract and was terrified of his wife. He only needed to hear her voice and his eyes would start to blink nervously behind a pair of thick lenses. His eyelids fluttered like the wings of the linnet that had once flown by mistake through the open sitting-room window of the Deelwaters' house and couldn't find its way out again. Aunt Harriet had sprung up and instructed us to open all the windows so it didn't break its neck on a pane of glass. The bird flew away, leaving behind two red feathers on the windowsill.

Nikolaus Koop blinked often in this way, and we had also noticed that each time he saw his wife he pushed his glasses up onto his forehead. Mira thought he was trying to evade his wife through self-imposed blindness, a sort of escape route, just like an open window. But Rosmarie insisted that, unlike the bird, it was not his own neck he was afraid of breaking but Frau Koop's. What we couldn't know at the time was that it was Rosmarie whose neck would be broken, and by flying through a pane of glass.

I worked out for myself some of what Herr Lexow was trying to tell me as I looked into his blue eyes and discovered the rings around his pupils, which were no longer golden but ocher. The white around them had now turned a little yellowy. He had to be way over eighty. And who was he now, anyway? My great-uncle? No, as my aunt's father he was my grandfather. But he couldn't be, that was Hinnerk Lünschen. He was quite simply a "friend of the family," a witness.

A few years ago, at a time when my grandmother no longer knew that I existed, my mother went to stay with her for a fortnight. It was one of her last visits before Bertha went into the home. On a warm afternoon the two of them were sitting behind the house, in the orchard. All of a sudden Bertha gave Christa a look that was exceptionally alert and insistent, and told her firmly that Anna had loved Boskoop, and she Cox's Orange. As if this were the final secret she had to divulge.

Anna loved Boskoop, Bertha Cox's Orange. In autumn the sisters' hair carried the scent of apples, as did their clothes and hands. They would cook apple puree, apple cider, and apple jelly with cinnamon, and more often than not they would have apples in their apron pockets and apples with bites taken out of them in their hands. Bertha would start by quickly eating a fat ring around the middle, nibble carefully around the blossom end at the bottom, around the stalk at the top, and then she would throw away the core in a high arc. Anna ate her apples slowly, relishing them from top to bottom—the entire thing. She would spend hours chewing on the seeds. When Bertha scolded her for this, saying that the seeds were poisonous, Anna replied that they tasted like marzipan. She only ever spat out the stalk. That was what Bertha told me when she noticed once that I ate apples like her, Bertha. That was how most people ate apples.

In summer, Carsten Lexow gave his pupils a day off because of the heat, a "fruit-picking day," as he called it. Bertha laughed and said it was the pick of her lessons. Carsten Lexow noticed his pupil's small white teeth and the fidgety ease with which her large hands tried to push the loose hair at the nape of her neck back into her pigtails. As her teacher was still looking at her, and because she felt she might have annoyed him with her cheeky comment, she blushed, turned, and slunk away. His heart pounding, Herr Lexow stared at Bertha and said nothing. Anna saw everything, she recognized the look with which Herr Lexow followed her sister, recognized it just as you would recognize your own reflection in the mirror, and hurried off to find Bertha, her cheeks a deep red and her head bowed.

Anna loved Lexow, Lexow loved Bertha, and Bertha? She actually loved Heinrich Lünschen, or Hinnerk as everyone called him. He was the son of the landlord at the village pub, a nobody with little land. All the family had were two small pastures right at the edge of the village, and these were leased to an even poorer old devil. Hinnerk hated his parents' pub. Hated the smell of the kitchen and of stale beer in the bar in the morning. Hated the passionate and loud rows his parents had, hated their equally passionate and loud reconciliations. One night when Hinnerk and one of his younger brothers—Hinnerk was the eldest—were forced to listen to a particularly ferocious argument in the dark kitchen, his brother said that they would probably have another brother soon. Hinnerk got angry; he hated all his mother's pregnancies.

"How do you know that?"

"Well, whenever they've had a row we get another brother soon afterward."

Hinnerk gave a cruel laugh. He had to get out of there. He hated it.

He had come to the attention of Herr Deelwater because the pastor and the old teacher had praised his intellect to the skies. Hinnerk was cleverer than anybody else in the village, he was very well aware of this, and a few others who were not stupid themselves had noticed it, too. Hinnerk was often at the Deelwaters' house. He helped on the farm at harvest time, earning himself a little money. He was given even more money by the pastor; however, this only made the proud Hinnerk hate this man, too. He quit the church at the first available opportunity, which was provided by his mother's funeral. They could save on costs for the homily, he said, anyone else could do it just as well, all those speeches sounded the same anyway, all priests did was insert the relevant name, but some of them found even that difficult enough. The pastor, who had put a lot of money into Hinnerk's education, and whose—admittedly not very extensive—library had always been at Hinnerk's disposal, was deeply offended, not just because of Hinnerk's lack of respect and gratitude, but also because Hinnerk had come all too close to the truth. But the legal exams were passed with flying colors and the young lawyer, by then freshly engaged to the Deelwater daughter, was no longer financially dependent on the pastor. The pastor knew this and also knew that Hinnerk knew he knew, and this was what irritated him most of all.

I remembered Hinnerk Lünschen as a loving grandfather who could fall asleep wherever he laid his head; he made full use of this ability. Sure, his moods were unpredictable. But he was no longer full of hatred; he was a proud notary, proud owner of a law firm, proud husband of a beautiful wife who made him a proud owner of a proud property, proud father of three beautiful daughters and proud grandfather of two even more beautiful granddaughters, as he always assured Rosmarie and me while shoveling proud portions of Fürst-Pückler ice cream into the cut-glass bowls. Everything had turned upside down: now he, Hinnerk, was hated by many, but he didn't hate himself anymore; after all, he had achieved everything he wanted. He was still the smartest man in the village and now everybody knew it.

He had even had a family crest designed in order to obscure his lowly origins, which was pointless of course: everybody came to him because he spoke the regional dialect, not because of his impressive family tree. So the framed picture of the family crest always stayed in the storage room, what had been the maid's room, where it still hung now. But I also remembered that whenever he looked at the crest the hint of a smile would play on his well-defined lips: satisfaction or self-mockery? I expect he was not sure himself.

Bertha loved Hinnerk. She loved his grim aura, his silences, and his biting sarcasm toward other people. But whenever he saw Anna his face would light up, he would smile politely and joke, and off the top of his head he would make up a sonnet about the bite Anna was about to take of her apple or a solemn ode to Bertha's left pigtail, or walk on his hands in the yard, upsetting the chickens, which scuttled away clucking. The two girls laughed out loud, Bertha bashfully tugged at the ribbon on her left pigtail, and with feigned serenity and a hidden smile Anna threw the remains of her apple into the lilac, for once refraining from devouring the whole thing.

In the beginning, Hinnerk wanted Anna. He knew that she was the elder daughter of Carl Deelwater; if she hadn't been he probably wouldn't have wanted her, at least not quite as much. But it wasn't her inheritance that attracted him, or not that alone. It was far more her status that he admired, her calm self-confidence, something he was totally lacking in. He could see her beauty, too, of course, her large breasts and hips and her supple back. He was charmed by the warm-hearted indifference Anna showed him, but he always took care to pay the same amount of attention to both girls. Was this calculation or respect? A fondness for Bertha or sympathy for the younger daughter whose feelings he must have been aware of?

My grandmother knew that she was Hinnerk's second choice. She had once said this to Rosmarie and me, without any bitterness, not even with regret, just very soberly, as if it had had to be thus. It was something we didn't like to hear, we were almost angry at Bertha; love shouldn't be like that, we thought. And without ever having agreed this between ourselves, we never told Mira.

Now that Inga was no longer Hinnerk's daughter I could better understand Bertha's lack of bitterness toward her husband, maybe her devotion to him, too. And with her it was always like the apples from the tree: they lay where they fell and, as she herself would say, they rarely fell far from the tree. After Bertha fell from the apple tree at the age of sixty-three, and then one memory after another came loose and fell, too, she gave in to this disintegration, forlornly and without a struggle. The wheels of destiny have always been set in motion—in our family as well—by a fall. And by an apple.

Herr Lexow spoke calmly, staring into his mug. It was now dark and we had switched on the wicker-shaded light that hung above the kitchen table. Sighing into his milk, Herr

Lexow said that one night, after a hot and muggy day, he had gone for a walk, which had led him past the Deelwaters' house, not totally by chance.

The house was in darkness. He stepped slowly onto the drive and stole along the side of the house and barn, straight to the orchard. Feeling a sudden embarrassment at creeping around like this, he decided just to walk over to the far side where he would climb over the fence into the neighboring pasture and cross this to get back on the lock path. But as he was passing beneath an apple tree he let out a yell. Something had hit him above his left eye. Not a stone, it wasn't that hard, but it was wet, and when it bounced off his head it fell apart.

An apple.

Or, rather, the remains of an apple. The flesh at the blossom end was missing; the top half with its stalk lay in two pieces by his shoe. Lexow stood still, his breathing rapid and fitful. There was a rustling in the tree. He looked upward through the leaves, straining his eyes, but it was too dark. Carsten got the impression that something large and white was shimmering up above. There was another rustling and the boughs of the tree shook violently. When the girl jumped from the tree and landed with a thud, Carsten didn't recognize her face, she was standing so close to him. The face came even closer and kissed Carsten on the lips. He closed his eyes; the lips were warm and tasted of apples. Of Boskoop. And bitter almonds. Before he could say anything the girl's lips kissed Carsten's once more and so he kissed them back, and the two of them fell into the grass beneath the apple tree, and breathlessly and clumsily removed the clothes from their bodies. Carsten's tree nymph was wearing only a nightshirt, so it wasn't that hard to free her from it, but when two people are trying to undress, undress each other, but also kiss and not leave each other's arms for a second, it isn't so easy, especially when, as in this case, neither of them is experienced in what they are doing. But they did it and much more besides, and the earth glowed around them so that the apple tree beneath which they were lying began to push out buds for the second time, even though it was June already.

Of course, Herr Lexow didn't go into the details of what went on beneath the apple tree, and I was glad of this, but his soft yet keenly spoken words—his eyes still fixed on his mug—evoked images in my mind that seemed familiar, as if they had been described to me before, as if I had heard them as a child, maybe from an adult conversation that I had listened in to secretly from a hiding place, and that I hadn't understood until now. Thus Carsten Lexow's story became part of my own story and part of my story about the story of my grandmother and part of my story about the story of my grandmother's story of Great-Aunt Anna.

Whether Carsten Lexow had cried out Bertha's name at any point and then pushed away the girl in his arms and run, whether during their lovemaking he had realized his mistake by her large breasts and taken his hands off her, whether the two of them went on right to the end as if they didn't know what the other knew, only afterward going their separate ways in silence, never to find each other again, I didn't know and probably would never find out. But what everyone in the village had talked about and what Rosmarie, Mira, and I often heard was the story of the old Boskoop tree in the

Deelwaters' orchard, which started to blossom one warm summer's night and the following morning was covered in white as if there had been a frost. But the wonderful blossoms were fragile and that same morning they had fallen to the ground silently, in thick flakes. The entire farmstead stood around the tree, awestruck, suspicious, delighted, or simply astonished. Only Anna Deelwater didn't see it; she had caught a cold, felt a slight burning in her throat, and had to stay in bed. The burning intensified and scorched the delicate cilia in her bronchial tubes, then spread until her lungs became inflamed and finally grew weak. Carsten Lexow never saw her again, and four weeks after the apple tree had blossomed she was dead. A tragic case of pneumonia.

Herr Lexow glanced at his watch and asked whether he should go. I didn't know what time it was but nor did I know what had happened next; we hadn't got any further in his story of Bertha. But maybe he should go. He saw my hesitation and stood up immediately.

"Please, Herr Lexow, we haven't finished yet."

"No, we haven't. But perhaps we are done for tonight?"

"Maybe. For tonight. Will you come again tomorrow evening?"

"No, there's a council meeting I can't miss."

"Tomorrow afternoon for a cup of coffee?"

"I'd love to."

"Thanks for the soup. And the milk. And for the house, the garden . . ."

"Not at all. Please, Iris, you know that it's me who needs to thank you and to apologize."

"You've absolutely no need to apologize to me. What for? For having loved my grandmother till the day she died, or for the death of my great-aunt Anna? Honestly."

"No, I don't have to apologize to you for that," he said, giving me a warm smile. I could see exactly why my great-aunt Anna had fallen for him. "I only need to apologize because no one in your family knew that I had a spare key, not even your aunt Inga. She thought all I did was stroll around outside the house from time to time, taking a quick look." He felt in his trouser pocket and for the second time a huge brass front-door key was put in my hand. It seemed as if Herr Lexow had a spare key to many things, I thought as I placed the warmed metal on the kitchen table.

I saw the old teacher and my grandmother's lover to the door. "Coffee tomorrow, then?"

He waved briefly and went down the front steps somewhat awkwardly, disappearing behind the roses as he turned to the right, toward his bicycle, which he had left on the drive. I could hear the kickstand of his bike dragging across the flagstones and shortly afterward the soft humming of his dynamo as he cycled out onto the pavement and past the hedge. Then I pulled off my grandfather's socks, took the key from the hook, and went outside to close the gate.

In the dark I walked over to the garden, where Bertha's ghost appeared in certain corners. Her garden was like those grotesque woolen figures my mother had kept in her wardrobe: gaping holes, rampant undergrowth, and somewhere the hint of a pattern.

Anna loved Boskoop, Bertha Cox's Orange.

What did Bertha want to tell my mother back then? What

did she remember and what things did she allow to become forgotten? What's forgotten never vanishes without trace; it always, secretly, draws attention to itself and its hiding place. The girl's kiss tasted of Boskoop, Herr Lexow said.

When, a month after the miracle of the summertime apple blossom, Bertha ran weeping through the garden, she saw that the red currants had turned white. The black ones had remained black. All the other currants now had the greenish gray-white of ash. That year there were many tears and particularly good currant jelly.

Chapter V

I WOKE IN THE NIGHT, FREEZING. I had left both windows and doors in Christa's room open, and now the nighttime breeze had chilled the air. I pulled the blanket over my head and thought of my mother. She loved the cold. In Baden the summers were so hot that not only did she have every reason to own an air-conditioning unit, but she turned it up full, took all her drinks with ice, and every few hours went to the chest freezer in the cellar to fetch herself a small glass bowl of vanilla ice cream.

But when it was winter the gravel pits, quarry ponds, canals, and channels of the old Rhine froze more quickly there than the lakes up here in the rain-soaked north German lowlands.

And then she went ice-skating.

She ice-skated like no one else; she wasn't particularly graceful, she didn't dance, no, she flew, she ran, she burned up the ice. My grandfather had bought her a pair of white skates when she was young. He was proud of his own skating skills, which were limited to a brisk forward movement and one that weaved backward. He could also make big circles by crossing his outer leg over his inner one. But he hadn't taught his daughter Christa all the things she did on the ice. She cut broad figures of eight by putting her hands on her hips and leaning into the curves. She would take a run-up and leap wildly into the air five or seven times with her knees up. With each jump she would make a half-turn and sweep forward or backward across the shining surface. Or she would spin around on one leg, her gloved hands thrust up to the winter sky, sprinkling her pigtails with ice. In the beginning, Hinnerk wondered whether he could actually tolerate this kind of ice-skating. People would stare, for it was certainly eye-catching. But then he thought he could detect envy in people's whispers, and so he decided to enjoy his daughter and her strange behavior on the ice. Especially as otherwise she was very polite, gentle, and motherly, always keen to make life pleasant for Hinnerk, her beloved father.

She met my father on the frozen Lahn. Both were studying in Marburg: Christa sport and history, my father physics. Of course, there was no way my father could fail to notice my mother on the ice. Small groups of people gathered to watch from the bridges above the river, people who couldn't fail to notice her either. They looked down at the tall figure, which wasn't immediately identifiable as male or female. The legs in the narrow brown trousers were a boy's, as were the shoulders and the large hands in felted mittens, and the short brown hair swept under a bobble hat—Christa had cut off her pigtails before the first lecture. Only the hips were perhaps a touch too broad for a man, the red cheeks too smooth, and the outline of her face, from her earlobe to her lower jaw and then down her neck, ran in such a delicate arc that my father wondered whether it described a parabolic or sine curve. To his great surprise he realized he was curious to find out how and where this curve might continue beneath the thick, bright blue woolen scarf.

My father, Dietrich Berger, didn't speak to the young ice skater at first. He just went to the Lahn every afternoon and took a look around. The youngest of four children, he was still living at home with his mother. As his elder brother had already moved out and his mother was a widow, the burden of being the man of the house fell on his shoulders. He bore it stoically, however, and didn't find it too heavy, maybe because it never occurred to him to think about it. Although his two sisters mocked and insulted him, and laughed when he told them what time they had to come home at night, they were pleased that he had taken on the responsibility for the family.

I barely knew my father's mother. She died when I was small, and all I recall is her stiff woolen skirt over a taffeta petticoat that made a singing sound when it rubbed against her nylon tights. Aunt Inga said she was a saint. But my mother said something different: yes, her mother-in-law had always helped other families out, but she had never kept her own household in order, seldom cooked, and she might have spent a little more time looking after her children. My father was terribly pedantic: he loved systematic orderliness, methodical tidying, and efficient cleaning. Chaos caused him physical pain and so most evenings he would clear up after his mother. The four children didn't develop any sense of mischief and wit from their pious and sober mother. My father learned how to amuse himself—if not others—only later, from my mother, long after he had actually dared to talk to her at the end of the Marburg skating season.

When the ice finally began to lose its luster and puddles were starting to collect under the bridges, my father plucked up courage, and after a fortnight of their circling around each other every day he introduced himself, saying, "On average, the kinetic friction coefficient of skates on ice is 0.01. No matter how heavy the person is. Isn't that astonishing?"

Christa blushed deeply and saw that the ice shavings on the toe picks of her skates had already melted and were falling from the bare metal like tears. No, she didn't know that, and yes, it was astonishing. Then both of them fell silent. Eventually, after a very lengthy pause, Christa asked how he knew that. And he replied quickly and asked whether she would like to see the Institute of Physics sometime. It even had a machine that made dry ice. "I'd love to," she said, without looking up, a strained smile on her red face. Dietrich nodded and said, "Good-bye," and the two of them hurriedly went their own ways, both quite relieved.

The following day, the Lahn had completely broken up, the soft chunks of ice, now a brownish color, were drifting to the riverbank, and Dietrich didn't know where to find the ice-skater again.

During the night the moonlight cast sharp shadows across my pillow; I had forgotten to draw the curtains. The bed with its three-part mattress was narrow and the blanket heavy.

My guilty conscience kept me wide awake. I should have called Jon some time ago; I might have thought about him at least. Now I was thinking about him. Jonathan—until recently my boyfriend, now my ex-boyfriend. He didn't even know that I was here, but maybe that didn't matter; after all, he hadn't been in the place where I was before I came here, either. He lived in England and that was where he would stay. But not me. When he asked me two months ago whether we might move in together, I had the sudden feeling that it was time for me to go home. Even though I loved his country very much. Yes, it wasn't my love for him but for his country that had kept me there so long, and that was why I knew I had to leave. And now I was here. Now I even had my own bit of countryside in this country. I refused to see this as a sign, but it helped confirm that I had made the right decision to come back.

When you lose your memory, time passes far too quickly to begin with, then it stops passing altogether. "Oh, but that was so long ago," my grandmother used to say about things that were a week, thirty years, or ten seconds in the past. As she said it she would wave her hand dismissively and her voice would be edged with reproach. She was always on her guard. Was she being tested?

Her brain silted up like a riverbed. Then the riverbank began to crumble, until large chunks fell crashing into the water. The river lost its form and current, its natural character. In the end it didn't flow anymore but just sloshed in all directions. White deposits in the brain prevented electrical charges from getting through, all nerve ends were isolated, as was the person in the end: isolation, island, England, gland, electrons and Aunt Inga's amber bracelet, resin went hard in water, water went hard with a hard frost, glass was silicon and silicon was sand, and sand trickled down through the hourglass, and I should sleep now, it was late.

Of course, the two of them had seen each other again soon after ice-skating finished on the Lahn. In Marburg, avoiding someone is practically impossible. Especially when you're looking for each other. The very next week they met at the Institute of Physics ball, to which my mother was accompanied by a fellow student, the son of my grandfather's colleague. Both their fathers would have loved to see them start a relationship; this meant that Christa froze in his presence, while he turned into a zombie in hers. On this one occasion, however, the evening was a success. Christa was so busy looking around all over the place that she remained calm. For the first time the colleague's son didn't feel his companion's iciness settle on his brain and tongue like hoar frost, and he even managed to tease the odd smile out of her with barbed comments about the first brave dancers. It was Christa who had mentioned the Institute of Physics ball to the colleague's son. And although at the sight of her lips pressed together he could hear himself floundering as he spoke, he'd still had enough sense to invite her.

Christa saw Dietrich first, but then she had expected to find him there, whereas he had no idea she would show up. So some of her initial embarrassment had already passed when he spotted her shortly afterward. His gray eyes lit up, he raised his hand and then bowed his head in greeting. He advanced toward Christa with determination and a spring in his step, and immediately asked her to dance; then again; then he fetched her a glass of white wine and danced with her once more after that. Christa's companion watched, perturbed, from the drinks table. While he was relieved that everything was going so smoothly this time and that he didn't have to keep talking to her, he felt that it wasn't quite right. He also saw with a combination of amazement, satisfaction, and jealousy that his companion was a much sought-after partner, and so decided to ask her if he could have the next dance. Which was the very opposite of what he had planned for that evening.

Fortunately, he was a bad dancer and my father a good one. And my mother danced well with my father; she was freed from her stifling shyness because he had already seen her on the ice. That and the fact that my father was almost shyer than her. So they danced together at all the balls in Marburg that season: May Ball, Summer Celebration, Faculty Dance, University Bash. When dancing you didn't have to talk if you didn't want to, other people were there and you could go home any time you liked. Dancing was basically a sporting event, Christa thought, a kind of pair skating.

Christa's sisters guessed at once that she had a secret. During the holidays, which of course she spent in Boots-haven, she was—like all women with a secret—always the first one at the letterbox in the morning. But her sisters' questions, which were sometimes penetrating and some-times flattering, just made her blush and laugh, or blush and fall silent. When Aunt Inga started studying history of art in Marburg the following term, both sisters went to the first semester ball. Dietrich Berger, together with a whole group of young men from his student association, had already been introduced to Inga. Inga had taken a liking to a tall, handsome sport student and she assumed that it was him. But when she saw that Christa didn't even glance at the high-heeled shoes that went so well with her brown silk dress, but went straight for the flat ballerina pumps, Inga knew exactly who it was: Dietrich Berger, just one meter seventy-six tall.

They got engaged that same year, and when my mother, twenty-four years old, had finished her much hated teacher training at a secondary school in Marburg, they married and moved down to Baden, where my father got a job at the Physics Research Center. My mother had been homesick ever since.

She couldn't forget Bootshaven and clung with every last fiber to the house that was now mine. Although she had now lived far longer in Baden than she had in Bootshaven, she nonetheless believed that in the south she was just passing through. The first of those hot, humid, windless summers left her in despair. Unable to sleep at night because the temperature never fell below thirty, she would lie in bed, sweating, staring up at the frosted-glass lampshade on the ceiling, and she would bite her lower lip until it got light outside. Then she would get up and make breakfast for her husband. The summer gave way to a paltry autumn, and this eventually to a hard, cloudless winter. All bodies of water froze over, and stayed frozen for weeks on end. It was then that my mother knew she would stay. In November the following year I was born.

I had never fully belonged in that place, down there in Baden. Definitely not in England, even though for a few years I had fancied I might. Not here either, in Bootshaven. I had grown up and gone to school in southern Germany, and that was where my best friends were, my parents' house, my trees, my quarry ponds, and now my job. Here in the north, however, were the land, house, and heart of my mother. Here I had been a child and here I had stopped being one. Here was where my cousin Rosmarie lay in the cemetery. Here was where my grandfather lay, and now Bertha, too.

I didn't know why Bertha hadn't left the house to my mother or one of her sisters. Maybe it had been some comfort to my grandmother that my existence meant there was another generation of Deelwaters. But no one loved the house as much as my mother did: it would have been natural to leave it to her. Then it would have been passed on to me at some point. What was she going to do with the cow pastures? I had to talk to Mira's brother about it again sometime. I was unsettled by the idea of discussing family matters with Max Ohmstedt. I would have to ask after Mira as well, find out how she was.

*

It was still early when I got up. Sunday mornings felt different, you noticed this straightaway. The air had a different texture: it was heavier and slowed everything down. Even familiar noises sounded different. More muffled and yet more emphatic. This must have been down to the lack of car noise, maybe the lack of carbon monoxide in the air, too. Perhaps it was also due to the fact that on Sundays you paid attention to breezes and sounds that you wouldn't waste a second on during the week. But actually I didn't believe that, because Sundays felt like this even during the holidays.

During school holidays I loved to stay in bed the morning after my first night in the house, listening to sounds from below. The creaking of the staircase, heels on the kitchen floor. The door from the kitchen to the barn jammed; it always grated as it was shoved open and banged as it was slammed shut. And the iron bolt, which in the morning was hung on a hook, would rattle as it dangled beside the door frame. By contrast, the door from the hallway into the kitchen was loose, and whenever the barn door was pushed open the kitchen door would jump out of its catch and clatter open in the draft. The brass bell by the front door clanged when my grandfather left the house to fetch his bicycle from the barn and ride to the office. He would wheel his bike outside, stand it in the garden, go back in, lock the barn from the inside, and then go through the kitchen, along the hall, and back out through the front door. Why didn't he go straight out through the barn? Probably because he wanted to bolt the barn from the inside rather than locking it with the key from the outside. It seemed to me as if he just wanted to rest his hand on the shining brass handle of the large front door and linger at the top of the outside steps for a few seconds as master of the house; then he would grab the newspaper from the letterbox, put it in his briefcase, walk down the steps, leap onto his bike, and ride off into the young morning with a ring of his bell and a brief, jaunty wave to the kitchen window. In any case, if he had slipped out to work unnoticed through the back entrance, it would not have fitted the picture that he and everybody else had of the notary. Not even when he was no longer in charge at work. Even then, until his dying day none of the partners dared take over his office, although it was the largest and nicest.

When he had gone you could hear the noisy clattering of crockery from the kitchen, women's voices, women's laughter, brisk footsteps, the banging of doors; but the echo in the high-ceilinged kitchen distorted voices so you could never hear what was being said. What you could quite clearly hear, on the other hand, were the emotions buzzing around the kitchen. If the voices were muted and deep, the words monosyllabic and punctuated by long pauses, there was worry in the air. If much was being said, and rapidly, in the same, generally loud tone, this was day-to-day gossip. If there was giggling and whispering or suppressed squeals it was advisable to get dressed in a flash and creep downstairs, because in that household secrets were seldom disclosed. Later, when Bertha had lost her memory, she no longer spoke loudly and the pauses between her words were of variable length. If they threatened to get too long, they would be sharply ended by other voices. Mostly by several other voices at once, which would rapidly swell to a clamor, and ebb away again just as rapidly.

This morning, obviously, there was nothing to be heard. I was alone in the house, after all. The silence reminded me of that other morning thirteen years before when there was nothing to be heard, either. Just the occasional rattling of a door or a cup. It was the sort of silence that comes only in the wake of a tragic shock. Like deafness after a gunshot. A silence like a wound. Rosmarie had bled only a little from her nose, but on her pale skin the slight, sharply defined trickle looked as if it were mocking us.

I washed my face and brushed my teeth in Aunt Inga's bedroom, put on my crumpled black dress, and went downstairs to make myself some tea. I found an array of boxes of tea bags, even a packet of cornflakes that had a slight taste of kitchen cupboard but at least hadn't gone soft. Probably from Aunt Inga's brief stay at the house. I still had some milk in the fridge from Herr Lexow.

I went out for a ride. As I passed the telephone box at the petrol station I remembered I ought to call Freiburg. It was Sunday, of course, but I knew that the answerphone in the university library would click in. I said I had to take three more days off to sort out matters here relating to my inheritance. Then I rode on to the lake.

It must have still been very early because the few people I met on the way, all of them dog owners, greeted me with the discreet, conspiratorial smile that real early risers—those who do it on Sunday, too—share with one another. It was easy to find the path to the lake. Like almost all the paths here, it went straight across pastures and through copses. At some point I turned right and rode on a cobbled street through a village consisting of three farms with barns, silos, and tractors, then the path continued around two hills, through pasture again, and right once more into the next copse. Then there it was. A pane of black glass.

I would look in the wardrobes for old swimming costumes later: I didn't want to become a public nuisance. But it would be all right this time, there was nobody here. Unfortunately I had no towel, either, though there were two or three huge chests full of them in the house. I whipped off my dress and shoes and headed into the lake. The shoreline was overgrown; there was only one place where it was flat and sandy. A tiny patch of sand, just enough for one person. I went in slowly. A fish darted past me and I shuddered. The water was not as cold as I had imagined. The soft ground squidged between my toes. I plunged in quickly and started to swim.

I always felt secure when I swam. The ground beneath my feet couldn't be taken away. It couldn't crumble, sink, or shift, couldn't gape open or swallow me up. I didn't bump into things that I couldn't see, didn't accidentally tread on things, didn't injure myself or others. You knew what water was going to be like, it always stayed the same. Okay, sometimes it was clear, sometimes black, sometimes cold, sometimes warm, sometimes calm, sometimes choppy, but its substance, if not its state of matter, always stayed the same: it was always water. And swimming was flying for cowards. Floating without the danger of falling. My stroke wasn't particularly beautiful—my leg kicks were asymmetrical—but it was brisk and strong, and I could go on for hours if need be. I loved the moment when I left the earth, the change in elements, and I loved the moment when I trusted the water to carry me. And it did, unlike the earth and the air. Just so long as I swam.

I swam right across the black lake. Where my hands touched the glass-like surface it instantly became wavy and fluid. Herr Lexow's story slid off me, all stories slid off me, and once more I became the person I was. And I started looking forward to the three days in the house. What if I kept it?

I didn't get out at the other side of the lake. When my feet started brushing against the leaves of aquatic plants I turned around and swam back. I've always been frightened when something touches me from below in the water. I was afraid of the dead stretching out their soft white hands to me, huge pikes that might be swimming under me, places where the water suddenly turned very cold. As a child, in the middle of the quarry pond I once knocked right into one of the large rotting tree trunks that appear from time to time, floating just below the surface of the water. I screamed and screamed and screamed and could not move. My mother had to fish me out.

From afar I looked over at my bike and the small black pile of clothes on the white strip of sand. And I saw that now there was a second bike and another pile of clothes. Placed as far away as possible from mine, but that wasn't very far, because mine were bang in the middle. And I wasn't wearing a swimming costume. Hopefully it was a woman. Where was she?

I noticed the black shock of hair coming toward me in the water, the white arms rising and falling rhythmically. No. It couldn't be—it wasn't possible! Not again! Max Ohmstedt.

Was he following me? Max got closer, at an incredible speed. He must have seen my bike when he went in, but had he recognized it? And the black dress?

Max didn't look up once, just plowed serenely through the dark water. I could have swum past him, got dressed, and ridden home and he wouldn't have noticed a thing. Later I wondered whether he hadn't actually been trying to give me this very opportunity. Anyway, now I called out quietly, "Hi!"

Max didn't hear me, so I had to shout louder. "Hi!"

And: "Max!"

He jerked his head up—we were now at the same point—pushed back the wet hair sticking to his forehead, and looked at me calmly.

"Hi!" he said, somewhat out of breath. He wasn't smiling, but he didn't look unfriendly, either. Eventually he raised his hand briefly out of the water and waved. A gesture that, in its indecisiveness, seemed to be part embarrassed greeting, part white flag.

I was moved by his seriousness and by his pushed-back hair that stuck straight up from his scalp. I couldn't help laughing. "It's only me."

"Yes."

We tried to act as if we were simply standing opposite each other, remaining as static as possible, but beneath the surface our legs were furiously treading water to prevent us from going under. We desperately tried to find a subject for a friendly but reserved chat. I was stark naked and he was my lawyer. All this was running through my head and it didn't exactly add sparkle to my conversation. At the same time I was frantically thinking of a way to make a dignified exit. A small nod and smile, not overfriendly, a "see you" and then swim on—that seemed to me to be the best strategy. So I took a deep breath, raised my hand in farewell, and in the process scooped a huge volume of water into my mouth, which made me choke violently. I coughed, gasped for air, thrashed around in the water; tears welled in my eyes, and my face must have turned a strange color, because Max cocked his head to one side, screwed up his own eyes, and watched with interest my dramatic behavior in the black lake, which had previously been quite still. A coot flapped its wings; I coughed again, dived down, and resurfaced.

Max swam closer. "Everything okay?"

As I went to speak I started by spitting water into his face. "Yes, of course everything's okay!" I spluttered. "What about you?"

Max nodded.

I swam briskly to the shore. I had to stop once or twice to cough. But when I glanced back before getting out, Max was swimming behind me; he had followed and he wasn't doing the front crawl anymore. My God! Did I now actually have to dash out of the water, naked and in the middle of a coughing fit? I pictured myself trying to pull the black dress over my head and shoulders in a hurry and—because I was still wet—getting stuck with my arms in the air. Blind and bound, as the dress was made of stiff cotton, I would fall over my bicycle, and when I tried to recover, the arm of the dress would catch on the pedal. And as I hastily hobbled away, still tightly bound, dragging a man's bicycle behind me, my plaintive, animallike cries would be audible across the lake and beyond. If anybody were unlucky enough to hear them their heart would freeze and they would never—

"Iris."

I turned around. At least I didn't have to tread water this time; my feet could touch the bottom.

"Iris, I . . . Well, I'm really happy to see you. Honest. And Mira loved this lake, too. It was—well, you know how she was."

"Because it's like a black mirror. I know." A black mirror? Had I just said that? Max must have thought I was seriously daft. I tried to look as if I had just said something very clever, and then asked, "How is Mira?"

"Oh, you know, fine. She moved away years ago. She's a lawyer, too. In Berlin." Max was on solid ground now as well. We were standing about two body lengths from each other.

"Berlin. That fits. I bet she's in some cool office, wearing black suits and black boots."

Max shook his head. He seemed to want to say something in reply, thought about it for a while, then said, "I haven't seen her for ages. After the death . . . After your cousin died she stopped wearing black. She doesn't come here anymore. We speak on the phone from time to time."

I don't know why I was so shocked. Mira wearing color? I stared at Max. He looked a bit like Mira; he had more freckles, which I'm sure Mira had bleached back then. His eyes were multicolored. There was brown in there, and something brighter, green, maybe, or yellow. The same heavy lids. I remembered them now. I had known his eyes since we were children, but his body was unfamiliar. It was now a whole head taller than mine and leaned slightly forward, white, smooth, not especially broad, but in good shape. I steeled myself.

"Max."

"What?"

"I don't have a towel."

He gave me a slightly puzzled look, pointed with his chin to his pile of clothes, and opened his mouth. But before he could offer me his towel I said smartly, "And I haven't got a swimming costume, either. I mean, not on."

Max let his gaze wander across my shoulders and I sank a bit deeper into the water. He nodded. Did I perhaps notice the hint of a smirk?

"It's fine. I wanted to swim more anyway. Take whatever you need." He nodded again and swam off.

What a nice, earnest young man, and so polite, I murmured as I stepped out of the water, and wondered why that sounded so cutting. I didn't want to use his towel at first, but then I took it and dried myself until it was wet all over. I put on my dress. And when I sat on the bike to ride back, I looked across the lake and saw Max standing on the other side. I waved briefly, he raised his arm in response, and then I set off.

Chapter VI

BY THE TIME I GOT back to the house, the air above the asphalt was so hot that it was shimmering and the road seemed to change into a river. I wheeled the bike into the barn where, as ever, a damp semidarkness rose from the tamped-earth floor and a chill radiated from the whitewashed walls. Max's pale shoulders in the black water. Eyes like bogs and marshes.

Should I look through the papers? Check the inheritance documents? Had I in fact kept any of them? Go on a hunt for mementos? Continue to roam through the rooms? Go outside? Grab a deck chair and read? Visit Herr Lexow?

I took an enamel bowl from one of the cupboards and went out to the currant bushes in the garden. I was familiar with the feeling of the warm berries, which you had to cup gently in your palm, as if they were blackbirds' eggs, and then, where the bunch hung by a stem, pinch it free with the fingernails of that same hand while the other steadied the branch. Quickly and quietly, my hands picked a bowlful. I sat on the trunk of a pine tree lying on its side and teased the milky golden berries from the green stalks with my teeth. They were both sweet and sour, the pips bitter and the juice warm.

I returned to the house through the hot garden. A large blue-green dragonfly darted over the bushes like a memory, stopped for a second in the air, and then vanished. There was the smell of ripe berries and earth and something foul: excrement perhaps, a dead animal or rotten fruit. I got the sudden urge to uproot the ground elder, which had spread unchecked. I felt compelled to kneel down and provide some firmer support for the young sweet peas—Herr Lexow must have sown these, too—which had twined themselves blindly around fence posts, flower stems, and grasses. But instead I picked a few of the tall bellflowers, closed the low gate behind me, walked past the outside steps and kitchen windows, and opened the door to the barn. After the blazing morning light of the garden I couldn't see a thing at first in the gloom, and the earthy cold that prowled under my black dress felt intense. I fumbled blindly for the bicycle and wheeled it outside. Then I cycled up the main road again toward the church. But instead of turning left I went right, past the small paddock to the cemetery.

I stood the bike in the forecourt, next to another man's bicycle, picked a few corn poppies to go with my bellflowers, and went to the family graves.

I saw Herr Lexow from a distance. His white hair shone out against the foliage of the evergreen hedges. He was sitting on a bench a few meters from Bertha's grave. It touched me to see him there, but also unsettled me. I wanted some time here on my own. When he heard my footsteps on the gravel he stood up with difficulty and came over to me.

"I was just about to go," he said. "I'm sure you'd like some time here on your own."

I was ashamed, because he had read my thoughts word for word, and so I gave a vigorous shake of my head. "No, of course not. Anyway, I wanted to ask you whether you'd like to come over afterward and tell me the end of the story."

Herr Lexow looked around anxiously. "Oh, I don't think there's any more to add."

"Yes, but what happened then? Bertha married Hinnerk—what about you? How could you get . . . I mean how could you get my . . ." Embarrassed, I broke off. After all, I could hardly say "get my grandmother pregnant."

Herr Lexow spoke quietly but emphatically. "I don't believe I know what you're talking about. Your grandmother Bertha was a good friend of mine and I never showed her anything but respect. Thank you very much for the kind invitation, but I'm an old man who goes to bed early."

He nodded at me; a hint of coldness had crept into his voice. Then he nodded at the wreaths on Bertha's grave, which had already wilted, and made slowly for the exit. So he went to bed early. Nothing but respect. I looked for

Hinnerk's headstone and for Rosmarie's patch of earth with the rosemary bush on it. Had Herr Lexow forgotten yesterday evening already? Was it only those people who had something to forget who became forgetful? Was forgetfulness simply the inability to remember something, or was it that old people never forgot anything at all, they just refused to remember things? Everyone must reach a certain point where they have too many memories. So forgetting was just another sort of remembering. If you couldn't forget anything, you couldn't remember anything, either. Forgetting was an ocean that enclosed islands of memory. It had currents, eddies, and depths. Sandbanks would sometimes appear and join up the islands, sometimes the islands would disappear. The brain has tides. In Bertha's case the incoming tide had come and swallowed the islands whole. Was her life lying somewhere on the ocean bed and Herr Lexow didn't want anyone snorkeling around down there? Or was he using her death to tell his own story, a story in which he played a role?

Granddad had often told Rosmarie and me the story about the sunken neighboring village. Fischdorf, according to Hinnerk, had once been a rich parish, richer than Bootshaven, but one day its inhabitants played a trick on the pastor. They called him to someone's deathbed in which they had stuffed a live pig. Brimming with compassion, the shortsighted pastor gave this pig its last rites. When it leaped squealing from the bed, the pastor was so distressed that he fled the village. Just before he got to the parish boundary with Bootshaven he realized that he had left his Bible back in Fischdorf. He turned back, but the village was no longer there. Where it had once stood was now a large lake. Bobbing in the shallow water by the shore was his Bible.

My grandfather always used this story as an excuse to mock the stupidity and alcoholism of clergymen. Not being able to distinguish between people and pigs, always leaving their stuff lying around and losing their way. All so typical, Hinnerk thought, and he sided squarely with the Fischdorfers. He didn't particularly like it when people were punished for their success.

Maybe Herr Lexow wasn't Inga's father after all. Maybe he just wanted to claim the best of what Bertha had to offer. Something that belonged to nobody else, either. In any case, Bertha had only ever loved Hinnerk. I had to ask Inga. But what else could she tell me apart from another person's story?

Hurriedly, I put my bunch of red and purple flowers on Rosmarie's grave. I couldn't see Herr Lexow anymore. But I'd had enough of the old stories. I marched with long strides back to the gate. Out of the corner of my eye I glimpsed movement between the graves. Looking more closely I saw a man in a white shirt sitting in the shade of a purple-leafed plum tree a fair way from my family's graves, his back against a tombstone. Beside the man was a bottle. He had a glass in his hand and his face was turned to the sun. I couldn't make out much apart from the fact that he was wearing sunglasses, but somehow he didn't come across as homeless, nor did he look like a mourning relative. Strange place, Bootshaven. Who would want to live here?

And who would want to be buried here?

I took a last look at the place where lay my great-grandmother, Great-Aunt Anna, Hinnerk and now Bertha

Lünschen, as well as my cousin Rosmarie. My aunts had already bought their plots here. What would happen to my mother? Could her homesick spirit know peace only in this barren boggy earth? And me? Did the owner of the family house belong in the family grave, too?

I quickened my pace, closed the small gate. There was Hinnerk's bike. I climbed on and rode back to the house. Then I fetched a large glass of water and sat on the front steps where I had sat two days earlier with my parents and aunts.

Rosmarie, Mira, and I used to sit here often. When we were little because of the secrets under the stones, later because of the evening sun. The outside steps were a wonderful place; they belonged as much to the house as to the garden. They were overgrown with climbing roses, but when the front door was open the stone smell of the hallway mingled with the fragrance of the flowers. The steps did not lead up or down, inside or out. Their job was to effect a gentle but definite transition between two worlds. Perhaps that's why when we were teenagers we had to do so much huddling on steps like this, or leaning in doorways, sitting on low walls, hanging around bus stops, walking on railway ties, and gazing from bridges. Waiting to pass through, trapped in limbo.

Sometimes Bertha would sit on the steps with us. She was tense, for she seemed to be waiting, too, but she didn't know exactly whom or what for. Mostly she waited for someone who was already dead: her father, then Hinnerk, and once or twice her sister, Anna.

Occasionally Rosmarie would bring out some glasses and a bottle of wine from Hinnerk's supply in the cellar. Although he was a landlord's son, he didn't know much about wine. In the village pub they drank mainly beer. He bought wine whenever he thought he had found a particularly good bargain, preferring sweet to dry, and white to red. Mira drank only dark red, almost black wine. But the cellar was full of bottles and Rosmarie always found a dark one.

I didn't drink with them. Alcohol made me stupid. Blacking out, shutting down, unconsciousness—I knew about all the terrible things that could happen when drinking. And I hated it when Rosmarie and Mira drank wine. When they became loud and laughed excessively, it was as if a huge television screen had appeared between us. Through the glass I could watch my cousin and her friend as though I were watching a nature documentary about giant spiders with the sound turned off. Without the sober commentary of the narrator these creatures were repulsive, alien and ugly.

Mira and Rosmarie never noticed anything; their spiders' eyes glassed over and they seemed to find my fixed stare amusing. I always stayed a little longer than I could actually bear and then I would get up stiffly and go indoors. Never since had I felt as lonely as on those steps with the two spider girls.

When Bertha was with us she would drink, too. Rosmarie would pour the wine for her, and as Bertha always forgot whether she had drunk one or three glasses she always held out her glass for more. Or she helped herself. Her words would then get muddled, she would laugh, her cheeks would turn pink. Mira was restrained when Bertha was there, maybe out of respect, but perhaps also because of her mother. It was well known that Frau Ohmstedt liked her drink. Once

Bertha had nodded to us and said what she always said: "The apple never falls far from the tree." Mira turned pale, took the glass she was just about to sip from and emptied it into the roses.

Rosmarie encouraged Bertha to have a drink, perhaps because it gave her a better excuse to drink herself. But it was also true when she said, "Drink, Grandma, then you won't have to cry so much."

Bertha drank wine with us on the steps for only one summer. Soon afterward she became too restless to sit anywhere for long, and by the end of the following summer Rosmarie was dead.

The sun was lower, my glass was empty. Now that I was here I could visit Mira's parents and ask after their daughter. I hadn't found out much from her brother.

This time I didn't turn into the village, but kept on going toward town. The doorbell still had the familiar minor-third ring from my childhood. The garden had become pretty wild, no longer the model of geometric topiary with its borders marked out in string. "Has your father been playing with your geometry set again?" Rosmarie would tease when Mira opened the door. Now the grass was tall, the hedges and trees hadn't been pruned, not for a while.

I suppose I ought to have guessed, but I was stunned when it was Max who opened the door. He was also astonished, briefly, but before I could say anything he smiled, took a step toward me, and looked genuinely pleased.

"Iris, I'm glad you're here. I wanted to pop by and see you today, anyway."

"Really?" Why was I shouting like that? Of course he had to come and see me, he was my lawyer after all.

Max glanced at me uncertainly. "I mean, what a coincidence. In fact, I hadn't planned to come and see you at all!"

His smile narrowed.

"No, no," I said, "I don't mean it like that. All I wanted to say was that I didn't know you lived here. But now that you are here, of course I'll take . . . erm . . . you."

Max raised his eyebrows. I cursed myself and felt my face turning red. Just as I was about to prepare my retreat with a witty remark, perhaps something along the lines of, "Erm, okay, I think I'll leave," Max said with a grin, "Really? You'll take me? I've always wanted that. No, don't be silly. Stay here! Iris! Come in now. Or let's both go outside . . . Actually, come through. You remember the way to the terrace, don't you?"

"Yes," I mumbled.

As I walked in embarrassment through the house that had once been so familiar, I became even more bewildered. This was not the house I knew. All the doors seemed to have disappeared. And there was no wallpaper. No ceiling! It was all just one large space, painted white; my sandals squeaked on the bare floorboards. There was a gleaming white kitchen and a large, tatty blue sofa, one wall with books and one wall with a massive but very elegant hi-fi system.

"Where are your parents?" I called out.

"They live in the garage. I mean, these days I earn more than my father does with his pension."

I turned around in surprise. I liked him!

"Hey, it was just a joke. My mother always wanted to get

away from here, as you know. And my father was ill—very ill, actually. When he recovered, they decided to travel as much as possible. They've got a small flat in town. Sometimes they come and visit; it's only then that they sleep in the garage. But my car's not that big, and so—"

"Shut up, Max—Wimp. Now, where can I go swimming here without you creeping up on me? Just tell me where you're going to be over the next few days so I know the places to avoid."

"Calm down! I'm just doing what I always do. It's not my fault that you've been studying my daily routine so you can appear under my nose without a thing on. And now you turn up at my front door and start haranguing me!"

Max shook his head, turned around, and went into the kitchen. He was wearing a white shirt and once again had marks on his shoulder; this time they were gray green, as if he had been leaning against an old tree. While he was busy sorting out bottles and glasses I could hear him muttering words like "cheeky cow," "character flaw" and "obsessive."

We drank white wine spritzers on the terrace. Of course, there was more water in my glass than wine. The terrace still looked the same as it had always done; it was only the garden that had become completely overgrown. The crickets were chirruping. And I was suddenly ravenous.

"I've got to go home."

"Why? You've only just got here. I haven't even asked you what you wanted from my parents. And, by the way, I haven't asked you what you've been doing and where you've been living, because I know all this from my files already."

"Really? Where does it all come from, then?"

"Lawyer's secret. I'm afraid I can't give you any information about my clients."

"Right, but someone must have given *you* information about your clients?"

"Yes, I'll admit that, but I'm not going to say who."

"Which one of my aunts was it? Inga or Harriet?"

Max laughed but said nothing.

"Max, I've got to go. I still want to—I mean, I haven't yet . . . In any case, I've got to go."

"Right, I see. Those really are compelling reasons—why didn't you say so right away? Perhaps you'd like to leave a message for my parents? And don't you want to know where I'm going swimming tomorrow morning? And would you like to have dinner with me this evening?"

As he talked he unscrewed the cork from the corkscrew with great concentration, only looking at me when he murmured his final question.

I leaned back and took a deep breath. "Yes, yes, I'd love to, Max. I'd really, really, really love to have dinner with you. Thanks."

Max looked at me without saying a word. His smile was slightly forced.

"What's wrong?" I asked, surprised. "Did you only ask out of politeness?"

"No, but I'm waiting for the 'but.' "

"What 'but'?"

"You know, 'Yes, yes, dear Max, I'd love to, I'd really, really, really love to, but . . .' That's the 'but' I'm talking about."

"There's no 'but.' "

"No 'but'?"

"For God's sake, no. But if you keep on asking, well . . ."

"There you go, there was a 'but.' "

"Yes, you're right."

"I knew it," Max said with a sigh, sounding satisfied. Then he jumped up and said, "Right. Let's go and see what we can find in the kitchen."

We found plenty in the kitchen. I laughed a lot that evening, maybe inappropriately for someone who was here for a funeral. But Max and his polite audacity made me feel good. He had so much bread, olives, and dips in the fridge that I asked him if he had been or was still expecting someone. He paused for a second, pulled a rather odd face, and nodded. Then he gave in and admitted that he had planned to invite me over because he was a sensitive man and he had frightened me to death at the lock and because he couldn't have guessed that I would suddenly turn up at his place. He smiled crookedly and spread leek puree onto some bread. I said nothing.

When I got up to go it was dark. Max walked me to my bike. And when I took hold of the handlebars, he placed his hand on mine and grazed the corner of my mouth with his lips. His kiss shot through me with a force that stunned me. Both of us took a step backward, me knocking over a flowerpot in the process. I hastily picked it up again and said, "I'm sorry. I always do that when I feel relaxed somewhere."

Max replied that he had also felt relaxed that evening. And we both fell silent, standing out there in the dark. Before Max could do anything, or not do anything, I took my bike and rode back to the house.

I didn't sleep well that night, either. I had to think things through.

Once again I woke up very early. The sun's rays were still feeling their way uncertainly along the bedroom wall. I got up, threw on my mother's golden ball gown, cycled to the lake, swam across and back; on the way home I bumped into the same dog owners as on the previous day, but not Max. Back at the farmhouse I made tea, laid some cheese between two slices of black bread, and put everything on a tray. I carried it through the barn and then out to the orchard behind the house. A few pieces of weather-beaten garden furniture stood there. I moved two white wooden folding chairs into the sun, putting the tray on one of them and sitting on the other. My bare feet were wet from the dew, as was the hem of my dress. The grass was starting to straggle, but it couldn't have been mown more than four or five weeks ago. I drank my tea with a dash of Herr Lexow's milk, gazed at the old apple trees, and thought of my grandmother Bertha.

After she had fallen from a tree while picking apples one autumn day nothing was the same again. Of course, nobody realized this at first, Bertha herself least of all. But from then on she often felt a dull ache in her hips and started forgetting whether she had taken her painkillers. She would be forever asking Hinnerk whether she had taken her tablets. Hinnerk would get impatient and give her a tetchy reply. Bertha got confused by this harshness because she really didn't know, and could have sworn she hadn't asked him before. As Hinnerk always rolled his eyes when she asked, she stopped asking but became uncertain about many things. She could no longer find her glasses or her handbag or the house key. She got muddled about appointments and all of a sudden couldn't remember the name of Hinnerk's secretary who had worked in the office for more than thirty years. All this made her uneasy to start with, then worried. In the end, when she noticed it getting worse and worse, and there was no one there to help her or talk to about it, when whole chunks of her life, not just the present, simply sank into nothingness, she became frightened. This fear meant that she often cried, lay in bed in the mornings, her heart pounding, not wanting to get up.

Hinnerk was now ashamed of his wife and started cursing her under his breath. The path from the kitchen to the dining room was a long one, and by the time she had got to one room she had forgotten what she had gone there to fetch. Hinnerk got used to pouring his own mug of milk every morning and buying a currant bun from the bakery opposite his office. Although he no longer needed to work he didn't like spending all day with Bertha, listening to her uncertain footsteps echoing in the hallway. She would meander up and down the stairs, crash about in cupboards, rummage through old things, pile them into heaps and leave them lying there. Occasionally she would make her way into her bedroom and repeatedly change her clothes. If they were in the garden Bertha would accost strangers walking past the drive with a broken but effusive greeting, as if they had been close friends for years. "Oh, there's that dear friend of mine," she would call over the hawthorn hedge, and the passerby would turn around in alarm to see an elderly lady beaming at them. Hinnerk was embarrassed by Bertha's confusion; it wasn't a proper illness with aches, pains, and medicines. This illness filled him with anger and shame.

My mother lived far away. Inga was in town and very busy with her photography. Harriet just floated above it all; she was always going through different phases and with each new phase came a new man, which made Hinnerk more furious than anything else. So from time to time he would call my mother and grumble about Bertha without mentioning his growing fears. Inga was the first to realize that Bertha needed help. We didn't realize that Hinnerk also needed help until it was too late. Meals on wheels were ordered. When Bertha had lunch she didn't want any stains on the tablecloth. If they appeared she would jump up and hunt for a clean cloth, usually without coming back to the table. And if she did return then it wouldn't be with a cloth but with a saucepan, a packet of rice pudding, or a pair of stockings. When she thought my sleeves were too long and was worried that they might trail in my food, she said, "You need to move away from there or you'll get burned." But we would roll up our sleeves, still able to understand what she meant. Later it became impossible, so she would get cross and stand up, or sink into her chair and cry without making a sound.

One of her social circle, Thede Gottfried, came three days a week to clean, tidy, shop, and go for a walk with her. At some point Bertha started running away. She might go out onto the road, get lost, and be unable to find her way back to the house she had grown up in. Hinnerk had to go looking for her every day; usually she was in fact somewhere in the house or garden, but both of these were large enough to make it a pretty big search. Almost everyone in the village knew her, which meant that sooner or later someone would take her home. Once she brought back a bicycle that didn't belong to her. Another time she slipped out at night; the car was able to brake in time. She began to wet herself, wash her hands in the toilet bowl, and flush away an endless number of small items: envelopes, rubber bands, broken pushpins, weeds. She would search in her pockets a hundred times a day for a tissue, and if she couldn't find one because a few minutes earlier she had fished it out and stuffed it in another pocket, she would become distressed. She had no idea what was happening to her, nobody talked to her about it, and at the same time she couldn't help but know. When my aunts or my mother came to visit she would sometimes ask them in a whisper and with a look of fear on her face, "What's going to happen?" or "Is it going to stay like this?" or "But it wasn't like this before, I still had everything, now I've got nothing." She was jumpy, wept several times a day, and her forehead was permanently bathed in a cold sweat; her frustration would suddenly erupt and she would spring from her chair and leave the room, only to wander restlessly through the large, empty house. My aunts tried to calm her, saying it was only old age and that basically she was fine. And although she was being treated by a doctor, the word "illness" was never uttered in Bertha's presence.

Hinnerk was six years older than Bertha. He seemed too young for a heart attack at the age of seventy-five, because he appeared to be in perfect health. The doctors hinted that it might not have been the first attack. But who could have noticed this one or the others? He lay in the hospital for a fortnight and my mother traveled up to stay with him. She held his hand and he was afraid because he knew that this was the end. One afternoon all he said was my mother's name, with that tenderness he was capable of but rarely showed, and then he died. My aunts stayed with Bertha when this happened. They were sad that they hadn't been able to say good-bye, sad and angry that Hinnerk had had a favorite daughter, that they had had too little from him—especially too little love—that all that was left now was the wreck of my grandmother, and that my mother could run away back down south, where a loyal husband and daughter were waiting to give her comfort and support. This sadness and anger made them say terrible things to my mother. They accused her of shirking her responsibility for *her* mother. My grandmother stood by, weeping; she didn't know what it was about but she could hear the bitterness and the disappointed love being off-loaded in the voices of her daughters. For the whole time that Bertha lived after that, and it was fourteen years in total, Christa had a very tense relationship with her sisters. After every telephone call and before every visit she was unable to sleep for nights on end. When, two years after Rosmarie's death, my aunts decided to put Bertha into the care home, they first asked Christa with a sneer whether she would finally be prepared to take her mother in. Inga and Harriet said they had looked after her for long enough.

Of late, though, the three sisters had tentatively become closer again. They were three sisters, they were over fifty, they had buried many dreams, they had buried Rosmarie, and now . . . now they had buried their own mother.

*

The grass between the apple trees was much taller than here behind the house. I really did have to see Herr Lexow again. He wasn't going to get away that easily. I drank my tea, ate my sandwich, briefly thought of Max and shook my head. What had actually gone on there?

The sun's rays became harsher. I took my tray and was about to go back into the house, ceremoniously—it was the only way to do it with my golden dress on—when through the trees I caught sight of the old chicken shed, the Hock as they used to call it here. Something red had been sprayed onto the gray render. I walked past the fruit trees to the shed, where my mother and her sisters had once played with dolls. Rosmarie, Mira, and I had used it as somewhere to go when it was raining. From a distance I could see only a red scrawl, but as I approached I could make out a word: "Nazi." Horrified, I turned around as if expecting to see someone with a spray can dash behind the elder bushes.

I tried to scratch away the writing with a stone, but it didn't work. When I bent over to pick up the stone I stepped on the hem of my dress, and as I stood up again the worn material tore. It sounded like a scream.

I went back into the barn and tried to get my bearings—my eyes took a while to get used to the dim light. Earlier, when I had passed the alcove where the ladders were stored, I had seen some large pots of paint. I opened the first one, but the white paint it contained was rock hard and cracked. None of the other pots looked much newer. I would have to sort it out later. Who had sprayed it? Someone from the village? Someone from the far right or far left? A moron or someone who was being serious? Forgetting was a family trait. Maybe someone wanted to jog our memory.

To take my mind off it, I went to my grandfather's study. I wanted to investigate his desk. There used to be sweets in the bottom right drawer. After Eights, Toblerone, and always several tins of colorfully wrapped Quality Street. I loved those tins, the lady in the gorgeous purple dress and the horse-drawn carriage. I found the man rather unsettling, with his smile and tall hat, but I would go into raptures over the lady's delicate parasol and the horses' dainty legs. And wasn't there a black puppy somewhere as well? The only thing that disturbed me about the woman was her narrow waist. Her beaming smile couldn't hide the fact that she might snap in half at any moment. It was impossible to look at her for long. The sweets would make our teeth stick together, and if you were unlucky all that was left were those with the cold, soft white filling. My favorites were the rectangular red ones, Rosmarie liked the ones that looked like golden coins, whereas Mira stuck to the After Eights. But from time to time, when my grandfather passed around the tin himself, she would take one of the dark purple caramel and nut ones.

The key was still in the desk cupboard. Hinnerk had never bothered to lock anything away. At any rate, no one dared root around in his study. His fierce temper didn't differentiate between colleagues and subordinates, granddaughters and their friends, wife and cleaning lady. And he wouldn't hold himself back with his daughters, either, whether their husbands and children were present or not. Hinnerk was a man of the law, which also meant he was the law. So Hinnerk thought. But Harriet did not.

I opened the desk and was met by the familiar odor of wood polish, paper, and peppermint. I sat on the floor, breathed in the smell, and peered into the desk. Indeed there was an empty tin of Quality Street inside, as well as a narrow gray book. I took it out, opened it, and saw that Hinnerk had written his name in the front in ink. A diary? No, not a diary, a book of poems.

Chapter VII

AUNT HARRIET HAD TOLD US once about Hinnerk's poems. Although she lived in the same house as her father, she never talked much to him and even less about him, so we found the poetry even stranger.

Harriet's way of dealing with her father was to avoid him. As a child she didn't freeze in his presence like Christa and Inga. And she didn't cry like Bertha. She fled. When he yelled at her or even locked her in her bedroom, she would close her eyes and go to sleep. Yes, she went to sleep. It wasn't a trance or loss of consciousness, but sleep. Harriet called it flying and said that every time she dreamed that she was hovering in the orchard and then slowly rose above the apple trees into the sky. There she would float once around the pastures, landing only when her father stormed out of the room, slamming the door behind him. Although Hinnerk had been beaten regularly by his own father, he never raised his hand to a single person, however livid he became. He would threaten beatings and "corporal punishment," as he called it, he would spit and froth at the mouth, his voice would crack and get so loud that it hurt your ears, he would sulk and go quiet, he could whisper the most terrible things, but he never hit anybody and was never tempted to, either. Harriet exploited this; she fell asleep and flew away.

Harriet was one of those girls who could never simply like something or find it adequate; she had to rave about it. She would go crazy over children and small animals. After leaving school she decided to study to become a vet even though she had no aptitude for the natural sciences. Even worse than her below-average grasp of logic was the fact that she would burst into tears when she saw a sick animal. Already in the second week of her course, Harriet's professor had to tell her that she wasn't there to love animals but to make them better. My mother told me about Harriet's first practical seminar, examining the corpse of a black-and-white rabbit, after which she had chucked her lab coat at the feet of the lecturer; with her lab coat, she had chucked in her studies, too. After she stormed out of the laboratory her rather stunned lecturer stared at the door, but she never came back. My mother always told this story in Harriet's presence, and my aunt would giggle her approval. I don't know if it was Harriet who had told it to her or a fellow student. Rosmarie liked this story, too, and my mother would always vary it a little. Sometimes it was a cat being dissected, sometimes a puppy, and once it was even a tiny piglet.

Harriet studied languages after that, English and French, and didn't become a teacher as her father had envisaged, but a translator. It was something she was gifted at. She had the ability to put herself completely into other people's thoughts and feelings—a born intermediary between two worlds unable to communicate with each other. She mediated between her sisters. Between her mother and the seamstress who came twice a year to the house. Between her father and her teachers. Because she understood everything and everybody, she found it hard to take a firm stand on anything. Anyway, Harriet wasn't made for standing: she used to hover instead. Hover above things, always with the danger of course that she might fall and crash to the ground. Curiously, however, these falls were seldom hard; she would usually come spinning gently back to earth. Although she looked a little disheveled and tired when she was back on the ground, she was always in one piece.

Harriet was the only one of the three girls to have something like a history with boys. Christa was too shy. Inga had her admirers, who were allowed to look but not touch—maybe they had no inclination to, either. Harriet wasn't an especially artful or passionate lover, but she only had to be looked at in a particular way and she would get butterflies in her stomach. She let herself be carried along without any resistance and she was capable of experiencing such intense pleasure that it simply took boys' breath away. She might not have been good in bed, whatever that is supposed to mean, but she made men feel that *they* were. And that was almost better. What was more, as the youngest of the sisters, she also got caught up in that time when flowers, sex, and peace suddenly became very important. Not in Bootshaven and certainly not in the house in Geestestrasse. Unlike Christa and Inga, Harriet studied in Göttingen, kept a few Indian blouses in her wardrobe, and loved wearing flared trousers made out of nothing but large, rectangular patches of leather, all the same size. And she began to color her chestnut-brown hair with henna. Harriet was probably a hippie, but there was no radical change, no shift in her personality. She became what she already was.

Although there were only three years between Inga and Harriet, and five between Christa and Harriet, this gap seemed like an entire generation. And yet, because Harriet came from the family she came from, she lived her hippie existence in moderation. She didn't take hard drugs; at most she would drink some hash tea, but she didn't particularly like it and it made her feel hungry more than anything. Her doped-up mind didn't have the time to spread its wings and glide over the horizon, as Harriet permanently needed to fill her belly with food. She lived with another girl, Cornelia. She was older than Harriet, serious and very shy. There was no question of having men over. There were few men anyway.

But one day this medical student arrived: Friedrich Quast. Aunt Inga had told me about him only a few years back, on the same evening she had shown me the portraits of Bertha. I suspect it was because of Aunt Inga's bewitching voice and the way she filled her tales with suspense that I couldn't help but paint Harriet's love story in rich colors.

Friedrich Quast had red hair and white skin that shimmered blue in places. He was tight-lipped and withdrawn. It was only his powerful, freckled hands that seemed lively and confident and knew exactly where they wanted to go and, most of all, what they had to do when they got there. Harriet was smitten; this was something entirely different from the hasty and clumsy, albeit tender, caresses of her previous admirers.

She had first seen him at a friend's party; he lived with this friend's brother. He was standing alone, detached, watching the guests. Harriet found him arrogant and ugly. He was tall and thin with a long nose that curved like a beak. He was leaning against the wall as if his crane's legs couldn't quite support his body.

When Harriet left to go home he was standing outside the front door, smoking. Without saying a word he offered her a cigarette, which the inquisitive and flattered Harriet accepted. But when he gave her a light, stroking her cheek with his hand as he sheltered the match from the wind, not even pretending it was an accident, she went weak at the knees.

She took him home—that's to say, as she walked he simply walked along beside her. It was clear to both of them that he wasn't walking her home because he was a gentleman. It was Friday evening and Cornelia had gone back to her parents," as she did every weekend. Friedrich Quast and Harriet spent two nights and two days in Harriet's flat. As monosyllabic and aloof as Friedrich was when he was dressed, he became full of enthusiasm and imagination when he lay in bed naked next to Harriet. His beautiful hands stroked, held, scratched, and caressed her body with an assertiveness that over-whelmed her. He seemed to know her body far better than she did herself. Friedrich licked and sniffed and explored everything about her with an interest and curiosity that was not a little boy's joy of discovery but the appreciative con-centration of a gourmand.

Harriet remembered that weekend as the occasion on which she learned the most about herself. Her sexual lib-eration had less to do with the sixties than with these two nights and days. When she and Friedrich Quast weren't in bed with each other, they ate rolls and apples, which Harriet always had in the house. Friedrich smoked. They didn't talk much. Although he was a medic they didn't speak about contraception, either. Harriet didn't even think about it. On Sunday afternoon, Friedrich Quast got up and bent over Harriet, who gazed up at him in surprise. He looked into her eyes, said he had to go, gave her a fleeting but warm kiss, put a cigarette between his lips, and vanished. Harriet stayed in bed and was not much troubled. She heard Cornelia enter the stairwell. Heard her footstep pause for a second, a few murmured words, then she heard Friedrich hurry down the stairs, and only some time after this Cornelia's measured tread as she made her way up. Christ, Harriet thought. Oh Christ. And sure enough, it wasn't long before there was a knock at her door. Cornelia was horrified to find Harriet in bed in the middle of the day, hair tangled, cheeks flushed, lips red and sore looking. The smell of smoke and sex hit her like a slap, and she opened her mouth a few times to speak, looked at Harriet almost hatefully, and closed the door behind her. Harriet felt bad, but not as bad as she had expected.

However, she felt much worse than she had expected when Friedrich failed to call the next day, or the one after that. She spent the following weekend in bed, too, alone this time and so terribly unhappy that Cornelia started to worry and almost hoped that the man would show up again soon. Another week passed, during which Harriet had found out where he lived and sent him two letters. Then that Saturday evening her doorbell rang. When she saw who it was she vomited. Friedrich took her head in his hands, helped her back to bed, opened the window, smoked, and waited until the color had returned to her cheeks. Then he went over to her and placed his hand on her left breast. Harriet began breathing faster.

He stayed until Monday morning. Because of the pain she had suffered over the two weeks that he was away, everything was even more intense than the first time. Now she understood the meaning of the word "passion." When he left, a very nervous Harriet asked whether he would come back. He gave a brief nod and disappeared. Again for two weeks.

Harriet tried to pull herself together, but it didn't work; as the days passed she fell to pieces. And if she tried to hold on to one piece, another slipped off from elsewhere. And no sooner had she caught that one than the piece she had first been holding on to fell off. She got bad marks. Cornelia asked whether she might look for another flat. Her parents had a go at her because she had screwed up an exam. She lost weight and her hair dulled. When he turned up again a fortnight later, Cornelia stood at the door to Harriet's room and shouted that she would be moving in with another friend the following week. As she was in the middle of her exams, she was spending the weekends in Göttingen as well, and needed more peace and quiet. Harriet was ashamed, but her relief at seeing Friedrich again was greater. She asked him whether he'd like to move in with her. Friedrich nodded. It was a scandal. When Hinnerk found out about it he was furious. He went straight out and changed his will: he cut Harriet out. She wasn't to come home anymore. Not even at Christmas.

Friedrich lived at Harriet's flat, but would it really be right to say he had moved in with her? He slept there and left a couple of changes of clothes in Cornelia's old wardrobe. But his things, his books, pictures, pens, blankets, pillows—all the stuff a grown man might own—none of this was ever brought to the flat. Harriet was distraught. Friedrich, on the other hand, said he didn't need anything else. Harriet even went once in secret to see Friedrich's former flatmate, her friend's brother, but he no longer lived in the flat, either. He had finished his studies and returned to the Sauerland to start working for his father's firm. Nobody in the building knew anything about Friedrich Quast. When Harriet once asked him where the rest of his things were, he replied that his books were in a small room in the Faculty of Medicine where he was running a course for first-year students. And the other stuff? In storage. At the house of one of his mother's friends. Harriet became jealous. She had the suspicion that she wasn't the only woman he was seeing. Although Friedrich was indeed at her place more often, and although they always slept together whenever he was there, Harriet became more and more convinced that he must be seeing other women. Sometimes it was an unfamiliar smell, sometimes a letter opened too casually or a hasty departure after a furtive glance at his watch. Harriet closed her eyes. And flew away.

At some point she opened her eyes again and realized that she had been abandoned in midflight. Abandoned with a baby in her belly. Friedrich had noticed it before she did. Yes, her gums had bled quite often recently and once they had even been inflamed. Yes, she had also noticed she was tired, but that was down to the nights she spent having sex with Friedrich instead of sleeping. And the flying. She failed to notice her breasts getting bigger; she had perhaps felt something but didn't think any more of it. Friedrich didn't say much, he just looked at her and asked about her cycle. Half asleep, Harriet shrugged and closed her eyes. That night he woke her up, lay on her back, took her gently but energetically from behind, and left her flat soon afterward. At first Harriet wasn't concerned. It was a bit upsetting when he left but nothing unusual. Then she looked into his wardrobe, saw that even the few items of clothing had gone, and she couldn't help vomiting. And afterward the sickness didn't stop. She vomited in the morning, the afternoon, the evening and at night. As she kneeled over the toilet bowl in the bathroom she suddenly remembered his last question. Harriet screwed up her eyes as tightly as she could, but she didn't fly anymore. She hoped it would come back but didn't really believe it would. And her gut feeling—Harriet called it intuition—didn't deceive her.

Two decades later—Rosmarie had been dead for five years—Inga was passing a doctor's surgery in Bremen. She read the sign more out of habit than interest. And when she reached

the next crossroads the name that had been on the sign suddenly hit her. She went back. And there it was: Dr. Friedrich
Quast. Cardiology. Of course. A heart specialist, Inga thought
with a contemptuous snort. She was about to go in, but then
she reconsidered and rang her sister Harriet instead.

The pregnant Harriet wasn't devastated when she realized
she would have to bring up an illegitimate child on her own.
Eventually the vomiting stopped. She took her exams and
performed well. The glances and whispers of her fellow
students didn't bother her as much as she had feared; in fact,
there weren't that many whispers at all. It was only when
Cornelia, whom she bumped into by chance in town, walked
past her and shook her head at seeing the swollen belly that
Harriet went into a café and cried. After much deliberation
she wrote to her parents, and wasn't expecting the answer she
got. Bertha wrote back to her daughter telling her that she
would love Harriet to come home. She had discussed it with
Hinnerk and he wasn't happy about the whole affair. But—
and it was the only time that Bertha used this argument
against her husband—the house wasn't just Hinnerk's; it was
Bertha's parental home, and big enough for her daughter and
grandchild as well.

Harriet went back to Bootshaven. When Hinnerk saw her,
he turned on his heel and spent the rest of the day in his study.
But he said nothing. Bertha had got her way. Nobody ever
found out how high the price was that she had to pay for it.

Hinnerk refused to say a single word to Harriet during her
pregnancy. Bertha pretended not to notice and spoke to

both of them, but she got tired early in the evening, her blond hair detached itself from her beehive and she looked worn out. Her youngest daughter didn't see this, however; by then she had become totally inward looking. In the mornings she would sit in her old bedroom, translating. Thanks to the friendly assistance of a professor who held her work in high regard—or maybe he just felt sorry for her—she was working for a publishing house specializing in biographies. The genre suited Harriet and she found the translation easy. Thus she would type away on a gray Olympia up in her mansard, surrounded by encyclopedias and dictionaries, making one foreign life after another appear in a new language.

She would come downstairs for lunch. Mother and daughter ate together in the kitchen. Ever since Harriet had come back home, Hinnerk stayed in his study during lunch. Harriet washed up and Bertha would have a short lie-down on the sofa. Then Harriet would get back to work again, but only until midafternoon. She would stop around four, put a soft gray plastic cover over the typewriter, and push her chair in. By then her movements were labored and she would trudge slowly down the stairs. When she heard her daughter's footsteps, Bertha would push the beans she was chopping to one side, drop the heavy washing basket she was about to carry through the barn, or put down the pen with which she was doing the household accounts. She would listen in silence, clutching her neck. A dry sob would sometimes break loose from her throat.

Harriet noticed none of this. She would slowly make her way into the garden, take a hoe and weed the flower beds, for it was late summer. Bending over had become difficult. Unless she opened her legs wide to make room between them for her belly, all the breath was squeezed out of her, which was painful. Harriet got rid of the weeds nonetheless. Day by day. Bed by bed. And when she had finished she started all over again. Even when it was raining she would go over to the cow pasture where the washing would normally be hanging from the line and wade through the tall grass to the large bramble bushes to pick blackberries. The raindrops made the berries look even bigger, turning them heavy and soft. Juice and water ran down Harriet's sleeves. And each time she picked a berry the bush shook like a wet dog.

After an hour or two in the garden she would sit on an old folding chair or a bench, lean her head against the wall under the veranda or a tree trunk, and fall asleep. Dragonflies darted above her, bumblebees got tangled up in her red hair, but Harriet felt none of this. She wasn't flying, wasn't dreaming, just slept like a log.

But this meant she slept worse at night. It was hot beneath the roof, hot beneath the heavy blanket; her breasts sweltered against her swollen belly. She couldn't go to sleep on her front. If she lay on her back she felt dizzy. On her side, the ankle, knee, hip, and shoulder she was lying on started to hurt after a while. And then she didn't know what to do with her forearm: it would generally fall asleep before she did and that was uncomfortable. Every night Harriet got up and dragged herself down the stairs to go to the loo. But when she started getting up twice at night she began using the chamber pot she had used as a child, back when the way downstairs had been too long, too steep, and too cold to negotiate every night. Harriet didn't go straight back to bed after using the pot. The windows were open, but the cool air didn't get very far into upstairs rooms. Harriet stood by the window and the draft billowed out her nightdress like a large sail.

Rosmarie said Harriet had told her that people walking along the road below had seen a white ghost floating around the attic of the house. That must have been Harriet. She never left the property and so some people in the village never knew that she had come back. Most of them of course knew about her pregnancy, and gossip was rife.

It must have been around this time that the books on the upstairs shelves started being moved around. It happened every few months. Time and again all the books would suddenly be in a different place from before, and it always felt as if this rearrangement had not occurred at random, but according to a particular pattern. Once we had the impression that it was the shape of the books that determined the order, another time the texture of the covers; on one occasion we thought that the authors sitting side by side would have had a lot to say to each other, while on another it was those writers who would have despised each other who were close together.

But Harriet never admitted to it. "Why would I do something like that?" she asked her daughter and me, smiling at us in astonishment.

"Who else could have done it?" we asked in return.

"After all, you do fly when you're asleep," Rosmarie added defiantly.

Harriet laughed out loud. "Who's been telling you all this again?" She laughed once more, shook her head, and left the room.

I still wondered who had changed the books around upstairs. Had it been Bertha the whole time, even continuing it when she visited from the home? But now I was kneeling down here by my dead grandfather's desk with a bad conscience because I had found a secret book of poetry that he had written more than four decades ago. I put it back. I wanted to keep it for another time. And now I had to deal with the chicken shed.

I fetched my green bag with my purse, left the house, and cycled off. There was a huge DIY store on the way into the village. Without locking up my bike I went in and grabbed a large tin of paint. Two would have been better, but on my bike I couldn't manage more than one. I wasn't even sure how I was going to get that one back home. I also picked up a roller and a bottle of turpentine, and went to the till. The cashier, who may have been my age, gave me a hard stare and the corners of her mouth turned downward. It wasn't until I tried fastening the tin of paint to the pannier rack and the hem of my dress got caught in the chain that I understood why the cashier had looked at me in that way. I was still wearing the golden dress and the sight of the ripped hem—now with added black oil stains—failed to improve my self-confidence or lift my mood.

I shoved the roller and turpentine in my bag, hung it over my shoulder, gathered up the dress and stuffed it into the leg holes of my knickers to make it shorter. When I climbed onto the man's bike and pushed off, the heavy paint pot came within a millimeter of sliding off the pannier rack. I was just able to steady it, but as I did this I swerved dangerously, almost crashing into an innocent customer on his way into the DIY store. He shouted something after me that sounded like "Bloody junkie!" The man probably thought I spent the whole day sitting cross-legged in the garage with my friends, sniffing at one ten-liter tin of white paint after another. Shocked, I felt behind me, pressed the tin down firmly on the pannier rack, and cycled away one-handed and sweating profusely.

Just before getting home I turned into Max's road; I wanted to ask him whether there were still any of my grandfather's papers in the basement of the office. In truth, I just wanted to see him: my nighttime deliberations had produced no results. The strap of my bag was cutting into my neck painfully. The bag itself was being bounced from one knee to the other as I cycled, while the dress was gradually coming out of my knickers and hanging down in the chain again. But there was nothing I could do about that, as one hand had to hold on to the paint pot and the other the handlebars. All this was irrelevant, however, when a small black fly flew into my eye just before I got to Max's house. My eyes began watering profusely and I couldn't see a thing. A car was just parked there on the right—was that allowed? Probably yes, but anyway I smashed into it, let go of the paint and the handlebars; the bike overturned, the paint tin hit the road, and before I could cry for help, my bag with the heavy bottle of turpentine smacked me in the face, silencing me. At least it hadn't knocked me off my feet—I was already crumpled on the ground. Meanwhile, the impact had forced open the lid of the paint tin and emptied its contents across the road; paint was oozing into my hair and my left ear. Getting up was impossible, for somehow my feet as well as my bag had got caught up in the bicycle, not to mention my—once-upon-a-time golden—dress. I didn't plan on lying there for long; I just wanted to pull myself together, then rearrange my limbs and wheel the bike the short distance home. Then I heard footsteps in my right ear; not in my left one, which was by now full of white paint.

"Iris? Iris, is that you?" asked a voice somewhere above me. It was Max. I had the feeling I wasn't exactly showing my best side at the moment, and was just about to launch into a long-winded explanation when I started sobbing instead. Fortunately, this flushed the little black fly from my eye and meant I could stop blinking like an idiot.

While I lost myself in this and other thoughts, Max untangled my dress from the bicycle and unhooked my bag strap from the handlebars. He freed my feet from the frame and took the bag off my face. He leaned the bike against the hedge by his house and crouched on the road next to me. But if I had expected that Max would then take me in his strong arms and carry me off into the sunset I was very much mistaken. Perhaps he didn't want to get his smart blue shirt smeared with white paint. I gingerly picked myself up; it wasn't too difficult now that the bike had been lifted away.

"Can you walk? What hurts?"

Everything hurt, but I could walk. He took my elbow and guided me into his garden, having first thrown the empty paint pot in the dustbin.

"Sit down, Iris."

"But I—"

"No buts. This time," he added with a crooked smile. But I could see from his eyes that my expression worried him.

"Max, please let me use your bathroom and get this stuff off before it sets on my skin forever."

These words, which I said without sobbing or blinking like an idiot, seemed to reassure him. He said, "Okay, wait. I'll come with you."

"What for?"

"For God's sake, Iris, stop making such a fuss."

I sat down on the closed toilet seat and let him do it. He wiped around my ear and cheek so tenderly and gently that I couldn't help crying again. When Max saw this he apologized for having hurt me. Which only made me sob more. He put down the sponge, kneeled beside me on the bathroom tiles, and took me in his arms. That was the end of his smart blue shirt.

For a while I continued sniveling into his collar, but only because it smelled so good and felt so comfortable as well, and then he examined the grazes on my hands and knees. There were none on my face: I had been saved by my bag. Surprisingly, even the bottle of turpentine was still intact. Then he went out, and I got into the shower and washed the rest of the white paint out of my hair with a blue shampoo for men.

When I came back out to the terrace in a blue dressing gown—the golden dress was no longer recognizable as such—he was lounging in a deck chair reading the paper. A large number of documents were piled up beside him. Of course, today was a normal working day; how could I have assumed that he would be at home?

"Why aren't you at the office?" I asked him.

He laughed. "You should be glad I'm not. Sometimes I take stuff home with me." He put the newspaper down and gave me a critical look. "The paint's gone, but your face still isn't the right color."

I started rubbing my cheeks.

Max shook his head. "No, that's not what I meant. You look pale."

"That's your dressing gown. It's not my color."

"Maybe, yes. Perhaps you'd like to change back into that thing you had on when you arrived?"

I raised my hands. "Okay, okay, you win. I give up. Satisfied? May I sit down now?"

Max stood up and helped me into his deck chair. This was kind of him, once again, and I felt ashamed of my grumpiness toward him. I couldn't even explain it to myself and I started sobbing again.

Max said hastily, "No, Iris, it's all right, honestly. I'm sorry."

"No, *I'm* the one who's sorry. You're so kind, and I'm, and I'm . . ." I wiped my nose with the sleeve of his dressing gown. ". . . and I'm wiping my nose on your dressing gown! That's awful!"

Max laughed and said it really *was* awful and that I should stop doing it and instead take a sip of the water he had put on the table for me.

So I did as I was told and also ate two chocolate biscuits and an apple. Max asked, "What were you going to do with the paint?"

"Well, paint."

"I see."

He looked at me, and I giggled. But then I remembered the writing on the chicken shed and became serious. "Did you know that someone's sprayed the word 'Nazi' on the chicken shed in our garden? In red paint."

Max looked up at the sky. "No, I didn't."

"So now I want to paint the chicken shed."

"The entire chicken shed? With one tin of paint?"

"No. But if I'd put two or three more tins on the pannier rack there wouldn't have been room for much else, would there, hmm?"

"Look, Iris, why didn't you just ask me whether you could borrow my car, or whether I could get the stuff for you?"

"Look, Max, how was I supposed to know you were hanging around here rather than in the office?" And then I added, "Anyway, I was on my way to see you." I gave him a hard stare and hoped that he wouldn't notice that I was knotting myself up in strange contradictions.

Max wrinkled his brow and I kept on talking rapidly. "I wanted to know what papers you might still have in the office relating to my grandfather. Did a Nazi write that, or is someone trying to accuse us of being Nazis?"

"I'll have a look. We've still got some cardboard boxes in the basement belonging to the old man. But if there'd been anything incriminating in them I doubt he'd have stored them with us."

"That's true. So I must have just been coming to see you."

Max looked at me quizzically. "Are you making fun of me, or are you flirting?"

"I'm not making fun of you. You rescued me, and I used your blue shampoo for men and blew my nose on your dressing gown. I'm very much indebted to you."

"You're flirting with me, then," Max said thoughtfully. "Excellent."

He nodded.

Chapter VIII

ALTHOUGH IT WAS ONLY A short distance to my house I didn't want to walk it in Max's blue dressing gown. So I got into his car and Max put the bike in the boot, although only half of it fitted in. He didn't let me out at the bottom of the drive but opened the wide gate and took me as far as the green gate that led to the yard. He retrieved my bicycle from the boot and inspected it.

"Doesn't seem to be any damage. You're lucky."

I nodded.

Max scrutinized me as closely as he had the bicycle. "You ought to get some rest."

I nodded again, thanked him, and walked through the garden to the front door, trying to look dignified and poised in spite of the huge dressing gown. I must have succeeded, because when I reached the corner of the house and turned to Max, I could see him watching me with his arms folded. I couldn't read his expression but I tried to persuade myself that it was full of wonder.

By now it must have been the afternoon. I slipped off my sandals at the bottom of the staircase and hauled myself up, groaning a duet with the banisters. Everything was still hurting. The shock. I threw myself on the bed and fell asleep instantaneously.

Something rang, twice, three times; I wasn't yet properly awake before it had stopped. I struggled my way out from dreams and bedcovers, and suddenly heard the staircase cracking and creaking. I started and the first thing I saw was Max's shock of brown hair through the banisters, followed by his shoulders. When the whole of him had arrived upstairs he found me at the door to Inga's room.

"Iris? Please don't be alarmed."

I was not in the least alarmed; in fact I was very pleased to see him. Even though it was a mess up here and I still had his dressing gown on.

I smiled and said, "Is this a ploy of yours, sneaking up on women when they're lying about defenselessly somewhere?"

"You didn't hear me ring. I just wanted to check on you— it's six o'clock. And when no one answered I was worried that you might be feeling ill. So I just came in—the front door wasn't locked. And I've also brought some paint, a brush, and a roller. It's all downstairs."

I realized that I was feeling fine. My hands were still stinging a bit, my knees, too, but the exhaustion had passed and my head was clear. "I'm fine. Really good, in fact. How lovely that you're here. Right, now get out: as you say it's six o'clock and I've worn nothing sensible all day."

Max cast a long, thoughtful look at his dressing gown. "You haven't got anything on underneath, have you. Is that a ploy of *yours*?"

"Hey, out I said!"

"Because if it is a ploy, then I have to tell you it's working."

"Look away, Wimp."

"Okay, I'm going. But I do feel that it's only my right to look at my own dressing gown. After all, I'd like to make sure you're not wiping your nose on it."

"Out!"

Max ducked instinctively when I threw a cushion at him. Although he was already halfway out the door he turned slowly to me, picked up the cushion, fluffed it, and leaned against the doorjamb. He just stood there, the cushion under his arm, saying nothing. In seconds I had goose bumps all over my body.

Max shook his head, tossed the cushion on the floor, and left the room. I shrugged off the dressing gown only when I heard him going down the stairs. Quite right, too.

I put on fresh underwear and was then faced with a problem. The black clothes from the funeral were too smart and warm; my second-choice black things were dusty and stiff with dried sweat. There was nothing for it but to root around in the old wardrobes. Harriet's pink-and-orange smock dress would have to suffice. Harriet's and Inga's clothes fitted me better than my mother's did. Hers were too tight.

When I came downstairs I thought Max had vanished. But I found him outside. He was sitting on the front steps, his elbows on his thighs and his chin in his hands. Three tins of white paint were standing on the next step.

I sat beside him. "Hi there."

Without taking his head from his hands he turned and looked at me through the crook of his arm. His expression was somber but his voice sounded warm when he said, "Hi there."

I really wanted to lean my head on his shoulder, but didn't.

His body tensed. "Shall we go and paint your chicken shed, then?"

"What? Now?"

"Why not? It'll be light till late tonight. And it won't matter when the sun goes down because I'm sure your dress will glow in the dark, too. It's actually painful to look at it in daylight."

"Loud, you mean?"

"Oh yes, that's it: loud."

I gave him a shove. He sprang up and fetched my green bag from inside. His eagerness was beginning to grate on my nerves. What was also beginning to grate was his avoidance of close physical contact. Coward. Or did he have a girlfriend? She must be a lawyer. She was probably at Cambridge in the middle of an MBA or MML, or even a KMA for all I cared. Spoke all European languages fluently, had doe eyes and a body that looked fantastic in tiny, sexily cut suits. I felt ridiculous in my fluorescent hippie smock and would have loved to send Max home. But now he was here with three tins of paint, waiting patiently for me to take the roller out of my bag. What about me? I had just napped for nigh on two and a half hours and wouldn't be able to get to sleep again before midnight anyway. Why not go and paint the chicken shed?

I picked up a pot of paint and the two rollers. Max stuck the brush in his back trouser pocket and took a pot in either hand and we traipsed around the side of the house. Past the kitchen garden where the smell of onions wafted up to our noses, then past the pine copse into which the evening sun cast bizarre shadows, until we finally got to the chicken shed. Back here the grass had not been mown for a very, very long time. Bertha used to keep the grass in front of the house short with her lawnmower, but behind the house Hinnerk would swing his scythe. As a child I loved the swishing sound as the grasses and buttercups fell. He would make his way slowly and calmly across the meadow. He didn't wield his scythe in wild sweeps but rather with the rhythm and evenness of a baroque dance.

"Here it is." We were by the wall with the red graffiti. "Max, do you know what? I think it's true."

"What's true?"

"That he was one. A Nazi."

"Was he in the party?"

"Yes. What about your granddad?"

"No, mine was a communist."

"But my grandfather wasn't just a party member; he always had to make decisions."

"I see."

"Harriet used to tell us things sometimes."

"How did she know?"

"No idea. Maybe she asked him. Or my grandmother told her."

Max shrugged and opened the first tin. He stirred the thick paint with a stick he had picked up in the pine copse. "Come on, let's start painting. You get going there and I'll start here."

We dipped in the rollers and ran them over the dark gray render. The white dazzled. I pushed the roller slowly against the wall. The roof began just above my eye level. Thin trickles of white paint dripped. Painting was another form of forgetting. I didn't want to attach too much importance to the writing in red. I mean, it wasn't God who had sprayed it there but a bored teenager. Just a prank, someone painting the town red, so to speak.

The painting went quickly; the walls of the chicken shed weren't particularly big. When we used to play there, Rosmarie, Mira, and I, the shed hadn't seemed so small.

My grandmother's hands brushed over every smooth surface—tables, cupboards, chests of drawers, chairs, televisions, stereos; she would run her hands everywhere, always on the hunt for crumbs, dust, or sand. She would sweep what she found into a pile with her right hand and then brush it into the cupped palm of her left. She would then carry around what she had swept up until someone took it off her and threw it into a bin, down the loo, or out the window. It's a symptom of her illness, they all do that here, the sister in the home had told my mother. A ghost house. It was all apparently so practical and functional, but it was peopled with bodies whose spirits had forsaken them in different ways and to differing degrees. The good ones as well as the bad ones. They all brushed their hands along the smooth plastic furniture with rounded edges as if they were looking for something to hold on to. But this was a misconception: they weren't feeling for something to hold on to. If Bertha spotted a stubborn mark, even if it was on the sole of her shoe, she would scratch at it fiercely and doggedly until it came away beneath her fingernails, disintegrating into specks or tiny balls and finally vanishing altogether. Tabula rasa. Nowhere could you find cleaner tables than in the House of Forgetting. There they forgot completely, their minds wiped clean.

When Christa came back from visiting Bertha she used to cry a lot. If people ever told her that there was some consolation in one's parents becoming children again, she would get angry. Her shoulders would tense, her voice turned cold, and quietly she would say that it was the most stupid thing she had ever heard. Confused old people weren't a bit like children, they were just demented geriatrics. There were no similarities. Comparing them to children was enough to make you laugh, if you didn't cry first. An idea like that could occur only to someone who had never had children or a demented geriatric at home.

Those people, who had simply wanted to console Christa, would fall silent, shocked and often insulted. The comment about demented geriatrics was harsh and tasteless. Christa was being provocative and that astonished my father and me. We knew her only as a quiet, polite woman, determined, maybe, but never aggressive.

When I studied *Macbeth* at school I couldn't help but think of Bootshaven. The whole play was about remembering and not wanting to remember, about getting rid of stains that weren't there. And then there were the three sisters, the witches.

Brush, brushing, Bertha's hands moving over everything that was flat: the body's affirmation that it still existed, that it could still offer resistance. Checking whether there continued to be a difference between itself and the lifeless objects in the room. But all that—the sweeping, clearing, emptying—came later. Prior to that, these tables and sideboards and chairs and chests of drawers were full of or piled high with notes. Endless notes. Small square pieces of paper, cleanly detached from notebooks, pieces cut out from the edge of a newspaper, large A4 pages torn from a pad, the blank sides of receipts. Shopping lists, memos, lists of birthdays, lists of addresses, notes with directions, notes with commands printed in capitals: TUESDAYS FETCH EGGS! or KEY FRAU MAHLSTEDT. Then Bertha started asking Harriet to help decode the notes.

"What does 'Key Frau Mahlstedt' mean?" she asked in exasperation. "Did Frau Mahlstedt give me a key? Where is it then? Does she want to give it to me? Did I mean to give one to her? Which one? Why?"

The notes kept on multiplying. They would float all over the place. Because there was always a draft somewhere, they would drift slowly through the kitchen like the large lime leaves through the yard in autumn. The messages on the notes became increasingly illegible and incomprehensible. Whereas the first notes were things like the step-by-step instructions for the new washing machine, over time they got shorter and shorter. "Right before left" one simply said; this was still understandable. But sometimes my grandmother wrote notes that she then couldn't read, and sometimes she tried to read notes that had nothing legible on them at all. The messages got stranger: "Swimming costume in Ford"—even though they didn't have a Ford anymore—and then "Bertha Lünschen, Geestestrasse 10, Bootshaven," over and over again. At some point this became just "Bertha Deelwater," but by then there were fewer notes. Bertha. Bertha. As if she had to make sure that she still existed. The name no longer looked like a signature, but like something copied out carefully in neat script. A short piece of handwriting full of places where the pen had stopped, paused, and then started again, a mass of tiny scars. Time swept past and the flow of paper dried up completely. Whenever Bertha came across an old note she would stare at it blankly, scrunch it up, and put it in her apron, sleeve, or shoe.

My grandfather grumbled about the chaos in the house. Harriet did her best, but she had to work on her translations, and Rosmarie didn't exactly help keep everything looking orderly and tidy. Hinnerk started locking his study to stop his wife from making a mess of it. A baffled Bertha would rattle the door to his room, saying she had to come in. It was a sight none of us found easy to bear. It was her house after all.

In fact, I knew Bootshaven only in the summer when I was here on holiday. Sometimes I came with both my parents, but usually it was just with Christa. Once or twice I came alone. For Hinnerk's funeral we made the trip in November. But all it did was rain. I didn't really see much except for the cemetery.

What was the garden like in winter? I asked my mother the ice-skater, whose name sounded like the scraping of blades on ice.

In winter the garden was beautiful, of course, she said with a shrug. When she realized that this wasn't enough for me, she added that on one occasion everything had frozen. It had started by raining all day long, but then in the evening the temperature dropped and everything glazed over. Each leaf, each stalk had its own transparent layer of ice, and when the wind blew through the pine copse, the needles had jangled against one another. It was like the music of the stars. Each stone in the yard looked as if it were made from glass. Nobody had been allowed outside. They had opened the window in Inga's room and looked out. The next day it had got warmer again and the rain washed everything away.

What was the garden at Bertha's house like in winter? I asked my father, who must also have seen it outside the summer holidays. He nodded thoughtfully and said, "Well, similar to how it is in summer, just brown and dull." He was only a natural scientist, so nature was probably lost on him.

When I was there in the summer I asked Rosmarie and Mira. We sat on the steps, hiding short letters under the loose bits of stone. The garden in winter? Rosmarie didn't think about it for long. "Boring," she said.

"Deathly boring," Mira said, laughing.

When Rosmarie, Mira, and I were playing one of our

dressing-up games, my grandfather came past to offer us some sweets from the Quality Street tin. He liked us. He liked me better than Rosmarie because I was Christa's child, because I was younger, because I didn't live in the house with him, and because he didn't see me so often. But he loved flirting with the two older girls and they would readily flirt back. This pleased him and he became quite charming, so I also asked him what the garden looked like in winter. Hinnerk winked at us, looked out the window, then, after a dramatic sigh, turned to us and spoke in a deep voice:

> Winter sees the gray man come,
> The frost, my child, and ice,
> And if you fail to dress up warm
> You'll get a chill in a trice.
> You'll cough and sniffle and you'll sneeze
> And speak right through your nose,
> Now red and running as you freeze—
> The winter brings such woes.
> Alone there sitting on your bed
> Wiping your nose sore,
> That wretched cold inside your head
> Keeps all friends from the door.
> Alone in the garden, too,
> Your heart so heavy and sad,
> No friend will dare come near you,
> They fear your cold's too bad.

Hinnerk roared with laughter and took a bow. Bravo, we cried, more out of politeness than genuine appreciation, and clapped our gloved hands. Rosmarie and I wore white gloves that buttoned at the wrist. Mira's gloves were made of black satin and came to her elbows. Hinnerk went back down again, still laughing; the stairs creaked under his feet. Mira wanted to know whether he had made up the poem on the spot. I would have liked to know that, too, but Rosmarie just shrugged. Maybe, she said. He's always making up poems. He's got a book full of them.

By now Max and I had reached the graffiti on the wall. I rolled over the "i," he over the "N." Slowly we crossed each other's path.

"I'll finish along here," I said, "and you start with another wall. It looks funny with just one wall painted white, so we'll do them all. Won't take long."

Max took another tin of paint, opened the lid, gave it a stir, then took it around the corner to paint the side facing the copse.

"Max?" I was talking to my wall.

Max's voice came from the right. "Hmm?"

"Haven't you anything better to do this evening than to paint this shed?"

"Are you complaining?"

"No, of course not. I'm delighted, I really am. But you've got a life, haven't you? I mean, I'm sure . . . well, you understand?"

"No, I don't understand. I'd be grateful if you'd finish what you were saying, Iris. I'm not going to help you out here."

"Okay, fine. It's my own fault. I was just trying to be polite. I just get the impression that you're throwing yourself at me and my business as if there were nothing else in your life—is that the case?"

Max peered around the corner and looked at me through narrowed eyes. "Maybe, yes, maybe that is the case. And so now you're inferring with that pitiful little woman's brain of yours that I'm only hanging around here because I'm lonely and bored." Max sighed, shook his head, and disappeared again behind the chicken shed.

I took a deep breath. "So? Are you?"

"Lonely and bored?"

"Well?"

"Okay, I admit it. A bit, sometimes. But it doesn't mean I generally go looking for the company of strange women and start doing DIY jobs on their houses and chicken sheds."

"Hmm. So I should be taking this personally, then?"

"Absolutely."

"What *do* you do when you're not painting chicken sheds or working?"

"Oh dear, I knew that was coming. Not much, Iris. Look, I play tennis twice a week with a colleague. In the evenings I go running, even though I find it boring as hell. I go swimming when it's hot, I watch telly, read two papers every day, and occasionally leaf through *Der Spiegel*. Sometimes I go to the cinema after work."

"Where's your wife? By the age of twenty-five you lot in the country have usually already got two or three children with a woman you've known since you were both sixteen." I was glad that I couldn't see him.

"That's true. And I almost did have one. My last girlfriend—who by the way I met when I was twenty-two, and who I lived with for four years—moved away last year. She was a nurse."

"Why didn't you go with her?"

"She changed hospitals, even farther away from town than here. And before we could consider whether we should move midway between her hospital and my office, she had an affair with her boss."

"Oh, I'm sorry, Max."

"Me too. But what I was most sorry about was that somehow I didn't really care. The only thing that infuriated me was the doctor-nurse cliché. My heart wasn't broken. Not even sprained. I probably don't have a heart anymore; it's sunk into this boggy landscape."

"You had one when you were little."

"Really? How touching."

"When you pulled Mira out of the water. At the lock."

"But did that have anything to do with my heart? I think it was more a case of doing my duty. And I didn't enjoy doing it."

"No, but you showed heart when you never said hello to us anymore after that."

"I found you creepy."

"Oh, come off it. You thought we were great."

"Terrifying."

"You were crazy about us."

"You were just totally crazy."

"You thought we were gorgeous."

Max fell silent.

"You thought we were gorgeous."

"Okay, so maybe I did. And?"

We went on painting.

A few minutes later I heard Max's muffled voice again. "This graffiti on the wall—it's been sprayed either by someone who hasn't got a clue what he's writing, or by someone who knew Hinnerk Lünschen well. Because there isn't a far-right scene here in Bootshaven. There isn't any scene here at all, in fact. Unless you count the car-washing scene or the geraniums-in-concrete-window-boxes scene. There's so little going on here that sometimes I sit in the cemetery and knock back red wine just to make something happen. I'm a boring man and just intelligent enough to realize it. Typical!"

I didn't say a word. I didn't fancy trying to comfort him, nor did I feel that he was asking to be comforted. And anyway, what he said was sort of right. What did I see in this glib lawyer? The past, maybe. In some way it must be important to me that he still had this picture of me as I was back then: a chubby blond girl trying desperately to catch the attention of two older girls. He knew me as Bertha's granddaughter, Rosmarie's cousin, Hinnerk's "little lass." And even though Max, like all little brothers between the ages of eight and thirteen, vanished off our radar, he had seen us all the same. Sometimes Mira had to bring him over to our place; we wouldn't give him the time of day, or he us either, but I did notice how he watched us. I could sense that, like me, beneath the feigned indifference was a streak of desperation.

These days, I didn't know anybody who knew us as we were back then—besides my parents and aunts, of course. But they didn't count as they never stopped seeing us as children. Max, however, was seeing me now. What luck that he was so nice. I supposed that had to be the case, really;

Mira had bagged all the other attributes. She was wild, he was calm. She caught people's eye, he made himself invisible. She left, he stayed. Mira craved drama, Max peace and quiet. And because he was so nice we had never noticed him. Sophisticated girls never notice the nice boys.

But now I had noticed him and I wondered why. Death and eroticism have always gone hand in hand, of course, but apart from that? Because neither of us had anyone at the moment? I had left Jon because I wanted to "go home." Everyone knows you have to be careful what you wish for because it might just come true. Max came with the house. The house. A shared process of forgetting was as strong a tie as a shared process of remembering. Perhaps even stronger.

And this solved the mystery of the man with the bottle at the cemetery. Not much could remain a secret in the village, not even from me. No doubt everyone already knew that Max was standing here painting Bertha Deelwater's chicken shed.

And what had Max noticed back then? That day at the lock was one of the first days of summer. I recall dodging huge swarms of green flies as we cycled through the cow pastures to the canal. Rosmarie was wearing a slim-fitting violet dress; the headwind billowed the thin, sheer material of her puffed sleeves. Her arms shone white through the purple voile and it looked as if two sea serpents were growing from her shoulders. She had hitched the dress up to her thighs so she could ride her bike, and the clothes pegs were blown flat in the airstream. I must have been riding behind her, because I can still picture the freckles on the backs of her knees. But that may have been on another bike ride.

I am positive I was wearing Aunt Inga's green dress on that occasion, too. I remember feeling like a river nymph on the way there, and like a bloated, drowned corpse on the way back.

Mira wore black.

We dropped our bikes at the riverbank, took our swimming gear from the pannier racks, and ran down to one of the fishing jetties. I put a huge towel around my shoulders and tried to get undressed beneath it. There was no one there apart from us. Mira and Rosmarie laughed when they saw me. "What on earth are you doing that for? What have you got to hide?"

But I was ashamed of my body precisely because I didn't have anything to be ashamed of. Rosmarie had small, firm breasts with rebellious pink nipples; Mira had an extraordinarily large chest, which you would never have expected what with her baggy black jumpers and her narrow shoulders. I had nothing. Nothing to speak of. I wasn't quite as flat as a year earlier, when I had gone swimming uninhibitedly in a pair of bikini bottoms. There was something there, but it was strange and embarrassing and it felt fake. I didn't understand why in swimming pools the girls always had to get changed in a communal area, whereas the women had their own individual cabins. It would have made more sense the other way around. It's the things that aren't finished that need covering up. This is as true of works of art as it is of potato beetles. It was perfectly clear to me which group I belonged to.

*

We sat on the wooden jetty and compared the color of our bodies. We were terribly pasty, and although my hair was the fairest I had the darkest skin of us all: a yellowish hue. Mira was alabaster, Rosmarie blue-veined with freckles. Then we compared our bodies. Rosmarie talked about breasts and how periods made them change size. I didn't understand what she was talking about; in what periods did they get bigger and smaller? And was there a period in which mine might not stay as stunted as this forever? Rosmarie and Mira laughed loudly. I blushed and felt hot all over. All I knew was that there was something I didn't know that I ought to know; my eyes were burning and I bit the inside of my cheeks to stop myself from bursting into tears.

It was Mira who collected herself first and asked whether my mother had told me that once a month women lose blood down below. I was horrified. Blood. No one had ever told me anything about that. I dimly recalled something that my mother had called "the time of the month," but that had something to do with not being able to play sports. I was furious at my mother. And furious at Mira and Rosmarie. I could have thumped them. Bang in the middle of their wobbly, jellylike breasts.

"Hey, Mira, she really didn't know!" Rosmarie crowed in utter delight.

"You're right. How sweet!"

"Of course I knew, I just didn't know you called it a 'period.' At home we call it 'the time of the month.'"

"All right, so you must also know what you use to stop the blood from trickling out."

" 'Course I do."

"What then?"

I went quiet and bit the inside of my cheeks once more. It hurt and distracted me. I tongued the marks my teeth had made. I didn't want to let on how little I knew, but I didn't want to change the subject, either, because I absolutely had to find out more.

Rosmarie looked at me—she was lying down in the middle of the three of us—and her eyes flashed as silver as the scales of the slender fish in the canal. She seemed to know what was going through my mind.

"I'll tell you: tampons and sanitary towels. Mira, tell her how a tampon works."

I was unsettled by what Mira said next: hard, thick cylinders of cotton wool that you pushed inside yourself down below. Bits of string that hung out of you, and blood, blood, and more blood. I felt sick. I got up and jumped into the water. Behind me I could hear Mira and Rosmarie laughing. When I climbed back out the two of them were discussing their weight.

". . . and little Iris here has got a lovely big bottom, too." Rosmarie gave me a provocative look.

Mira snorted. "That comes from all the chocolate your granddad gives you."

It was true, I wasn't thin. I wasn't even slim. I had a fat bottom and big legs, no breasts but a round tummy. I was the ugliest of us three. Rosmarie was the mysterious one, Mira the disreputable one, and I was the fat one. And it was also true that I ate too much. I loved eating while reading. One sandwich after another, one biscuit after another, continually alternating between sweet and salty. It was wonderful:

romances with gouda, adventure novels with nut chocolate, family tragedies with muesli, fairy tales with toffees, knights in shining armor with Prinzen Rolle biscuits. In many books the characters ate at the happiest point in the story: meatballs and compote and cinnamon rolls and a ring of the very best bologna sausage. Sometimes when I was roaming our kitchen looking for food my mother would bite her bottom lip, nod in a particular way, and say that I should pack it in as supper would be in an hour, or that I should pay a little more attention to my figure. Why did she always tell me to pack it in when she was trying to get me to do the exact opposite? She knew how much her words humiliated me, that I would storm up to my room and wouldn't come down for supper, and later I would steal the almonds and cooking chocolate and take them up to bed. I would read and eat, and I would be an unhappy, mute mermaid or a little lord, I would be stranded on an island, run over a moor with wild hair, or kill dragons. With the almonds I would chew up my anger and self-disgust, and then swallow it all down with cooking chocolate. So long as I read and ate, it was fine. I would be anybody at all apart from myself. I just had to make sure I didn't stop reading.

I didn't read that day at the lock. I stood dripping on the jetty and froze beneath the gaze of the two girls. I looked down at my feet; viewed from above they jutted out white and wide from beneath my belly, and my goose bumps were bigger than my nipples.

Rosmarie leaped up. "C'mon, let's jump from the bridge."

Mira got up slowly and stretched. She looked like a black-and-white cat in her bikini. "Do we have to?" She yawned.

"Yes, we do, my dear. You come too, Iris."

Mira bristled: "Go and play elsewhere, children. Just give the grown-up a little bit of peace, okay?"

Rosmarie looked at me, her watercolor eyes shining. She gave me her hand. I took it gratefully and we ran to the bridge together. Mira followed slowly.

The wooden bridge was higher than we had thought, but not so high that you wouldn't dare do it. In midsummer the older boys jumped from here, but today it was deserted.

"Look, Mira, that's your little brother sitting down there. Hey! Wimp!"

Rosmarie was right. Below us Max was sitting on a towel with a friend. They were eating shortbread and hadn't seen us yet. When Rosmarie shouted out they both looked up.

"Okay, who's first?" Rosmarie asked.

"Me." I wasn't scared of jumping: I was a good swimmer. And even if I was ugly, at least I was brave.

"No, Mira's jumping first."

"Why? Let Iris do it if she wants."

"But I want you to jump, Mira."

"But I don't want to jump."

"Come on. Sit on the rail."

"I don't mind doing that, but that's enough."

"Fine." Rosmarie looked at me again and there was a glint in her eye. I knew at once what she was up to. She and Mira had been ganging up on me and now my cousin was switching sides. I was still annoyed about earlier and yet I felt flattered. I nodded at Rosmarie. She nodded back. Mira sat on the rail, her feet dangling over the water.

"Are you ticklish, Mira?"

"You know I am."

"Are you ticklish here?" Rosmarie caressed her back lightly.

"No, stop it!"

Rosmarie gave her shoulders a halfhearted tickle.

"Go away, Rosmarie!"

I moved up next to Mira and said, "Or here?" And I pinched her sharply on the side.

She flinched and screamed and fell from the bridge. Rosmarie and I didn't look at each other. We bent over the rail to see what Mira would do when she resurfaced.

We waited.

Nothing happened.

She didn't come up again.

Just before I jumped I caught sight of Max running into the water with a splash. When I came up again he was already dragging his sister toward the bank. She was coughing but swimming.

She staggered onto the embankment and lay down in the tall grass. Max sat beside her. They weren't talking. When I got out of the water and Rosmarie ran down from the bridge, he looked at all three of us in turn, spat into the water, got up, and left. He jumped onto his bike in his wet trunks and rode off.

Rosmarie and I sat beside Mira, who still had her eyes closed and was breathing hard.

"You're mental." She panted the words.

"I'm sorry, Mira, I . . ." I started crying.

Rosmarie didn't say anything, she just looked at Mira. When Mira finally opened her eyes to look at Rosmarie, Rosmarie threw her head back and laughed. Mira puckered her small red mouth—was it pain or hatred, or would she cry, too? Her lips parted, she gasped for air loudly, and then she began to laugh, quietly at first, then noisily, helplessly, piercingly. Rosmarie didn't take her eyes off her. I sat beside her, howling.

"Max?"

"Hmm?"

"That time at the lock . . ."

"Hmm?"

"I felt so bad. I wonder . . ."

"Hmm?"

"I wonder whether it had anything to do with Rosmarie's death?"

"No idea. But I don't think so—it wasn't even the same summer. That was years before. What makes you think of that now?"

"Oh, I don't know."

"You know what? Maybe everything had something to do with it. So maybe that had something to do with it, that and the weather, and what was sprayed on this shed, and a thousand other things besides. Do you follow me?"

"Hmm."

I brushed the hair from my forehead. We kept on working. It was still warm. The paint job wasn't very effective; you could still easily make out the red letters. Nazi. Hinnerk had often used the word "leftie" himself. You would have had to be deaf not to know that he didn't like lefties. He railed against those on the right, those on the left, all parties and all politicians alike. He despised the whole corrupt pack of them, something he never tired of telling those who wanted to hear it, but especially those who didn't. My father, for example, was one of those who didn't want to hear it; he was a member of the local council and at home he would passionately put to us the case for bicycle ramps on curbs, roundabouts at junctions, and the switching off of traffic lights at night on empty streets.

According to Harriet, Hinnerk had written the poems after the war, when he was no longer allowed to work as a lawyer. He was sent to southern Germany for denazification. My grandfather hadn't just been an ordinary party member. I knew from Harriet that Granddad had been a district judge. He was lucky that he didn't have to put his signature to any bad judgments. My mother, who often came to his defense, had said that he had acquitted Herr Reimann, the farrier and a known communist. As a schoolboy he had often sat in Herr Reimann's workshop; the sight of the glowing metal had both frightened and thrilled him. He loved the hissing and steaming of the water. And yet the finished horseshoes that came out of the water looked to him like waste products. They were hard, dulled, brown, and lifeless, whereas before they had been red, they had glowed magically as if they had a life of their own.

To begin with, Hinnerk had to learn High German at school. Christa said the teacher had asked the new children what the following sentence meant: "Never torture animals as a game, for like you they feel pain." Hinnerk put up his hand and said, in broad dialect, "I know how they feel." Hinnerk was fortunate because his parents had finally given in to the pastor's insistence and sent him to grammar school.

The war broke out straight afterward, Hinnerk's father was called up, but Hinnerk stayed on at school. So, my mother used to say, if the First World War had broken out six months earlier, Hinnerk would never have gone to school, would never have studied, would never have married Bertha, would never have had her, Christa; and I, Iris, would never have existed, either. I realized at an early age that school was important. Vitally so.

When the Second World War broke out, Hinnerk was already a husband and father, not a victory-hungry hothead. He didn't want to be a soldier, and he wasn't called up but was put in charge of a prison camp, which meant he would come home for dinner in the evening as usual. Hinnerk Lünschen was proud of himself. Nothing had been gifted to him, handed to him on a plate. He had got somewhere and it was all down to his strength of will, his intelligence, and his self-discipline. He was athletic, he liked wearing a uniform and he looked dashing in it. And he thought that most of the Nazis' ideas were tailored precisely for men like him. It was just all that stuff about *Untermenschen* he could do without. For him, being an *Übermensch* was quite enough. He detested people who had to make other people small just so that they could feel big themselves. He, Dr. Hinnerk Lünschen, the notary, didn't need to do that. Of course he sorted out the necessary papers so that his old classmate Johannes Weill could leave the country to go to his relatives in England. It was a point of honor. He had never spoken about it, but Johannes Weill had written us a letter when, via a roundabout route, Hinnerk's death notice had reached him in Birmingham. It was half a year after Granddad died. Inga photocopied it and sent it to her sister Christa. The letter was polite and aloof; this man didn't have any warm feelings for my grandfather. I would rather not know how patronizingly Hinnerk may have behaved toward him at the time. Nor do I know if my grandfather was an anti-Semite; in any event there was barely anybody in his life whom he didn't fall out with at some stage. But the letter stated quite categorically that Hinnerk had helped his school friend. It was a huge relief for the whole family.

He had his quarrels with the Nazis, too, of course. He hated stupidity, and many Nazis were far more stupid than him. He also found it stupid to continue fighting a war they clearly had no chance of winning anymore. Indeed, he came out with this one evening when he had popped into Tietjens' for a beer. A woman was sitting in the pub. Was she the wife of a man Hinnerk had sentenced or brought an action against? Had Hinnerk ever humiliated her? He was smart enough to gauge weaknesses quickly, and sharp enough to be able to come up with cutting descriptions of people, but he wasn't wise enough to resist the temptation to do it in public.

Frau Koop had once said that Hinnerk had had a lover in town, a beautiful dark-haired woman. She had seen a photo of her, one she had found in Hinnerk's desk. Rosmarie and I were more surprised by the fact that Frau Koop had peeked inside Hinnerk's desk than by the photo of the mysterious dark-haired woman. Inga claimed she knew the photo. It was a print from the photographs that were taken of Bertha's sister, Anna. In any case, Hinnerk said he hadn't recognized the woman at Tietjens." But she must have known him or at least asked about him, because she denounced him. And so, to the horror of the entire family, Dr. Hinnerk Lünschen became a soldier at the age of almost forty, just before the war ended.

Hinnerk hated violence. He had scorned and loathed his violent father, and now he was supposed to go off and shoot people, or, worse, be shot himself. He stopped sleeping and would sit all night long at his study window, peering into the darkness. The lime trees in the yard were tall even then. It was autumn, and the drive was covered in yellow, heart-shaped leaves. On the day before his departure, Hinnerk left the Nazi Party. And he got pneumonia.

In the train he had a high temperature and was very weak. He couldn't be shipped to Russia in such a state, so he stayed in a military hospital. Although he wasn't given penicillin he recovered. In January 1945, he was sent to the front in Denmark. There he wound up in a prisoner-of-war camp, and after the war was transferred to an internment camp in southern Germany. I learned that from Christa, who was typing up Bertha's letters to Hinnerk and had read them out to my father and me. Bertha wrote about the pig she had bought and taken to the farm owned by Hinnerk's sister, Emma. And of all the pigs that her sister-in-law had, it was only Bertha's pig that died. What bad luck. Not that she could have recognized her pig among all the others, no, but she had to believe Emma. What else could she do? She wrote all this to Hinnerk. And about how she had cycled in the snow to a man who owed Bertha's father a favor. She borrowed an ax from this man because hers was broken. Bertha labored and managed to keep her family alive. They still had

Ursel, the cow. Strangers came into the home, refugees from East Prussia who were housed there. That was hard, Bertha wrote, having to share the kitchen. After the war, British soldiers were billeted at the house, too. They made fires in the kitchen, just like that, in the middle of the floor. They were awfully loud, but friendly to the children. Bertha wrote of the stream of refugees that flowed down the main road. The girls stood at the fence, watching hundreds of people with horses and bags and handcarts and baskets pass by the house every day. They found it very exciting. For weeks on end they loaded everything they could find in the house into two-year-old Harriet's pram, put on whatever they could find in the wardrobes, and hobbled in single file across the yard. "We're playing refugees," they explained to their mother, and out of necessity they had to stay in the chicken shed. Bertha wrote about this to her husband. She traveled the length of Germany to visit him. Without the children.

And then he came back. He didn't seem to be distressed, angry, or ill. He seemed no different from before: no moodier, no milder. Hinnerk was simply happy to be home. He wanted everything to be as it had been before, and so he pulled himself back together. The only difference was that from now on he called his youngest daughter, Harriet, who had still been a baby when he left, Fjodor. Nobody knew why. Who was Fjodor? Christa and Inga imagined that Fjodor must have been a small Russian boy with slanting bright blue eyes and shaggy dark hair. He had saved my grandfather's life by hiding him in his tree house and giving him crusts of bread. But Hinnerk had never got as far as Russia, of course.

After Hinnerk's return, Bertha went back without a murmur to playing the dutiful wife. She showed him the household accounts, which he checked. She let him decide whether to keep or sell Ursel. He wanted to keep her even though she was barely producing milk anymore. There were still strangers living on the upstairs floor of the house. Hinnerk didn't like this. He railed against the elderly couple even when they were in earshot. All of a sudden it was too much of a squeeze, and Bertha, who up till then had shared the kitchen perfectly well with this couple, had to draw up new schedules of who could be where when. She was ashamed, but she did it nonetheless.

Although Hinnerk had left the party he had been a district judge. He had accepted an important post in the Nazi regime and thus lost his license to work as a lawyer. The Americans soon sent him to a denazification camp. My mother told me that every few months she and her sisters had had to put on their best clothes. Then they would take the train to Darmstadt to visit their father. When Inga, eight at the time, asked him what he got up to all day long, he just looked at her and said nothing.

On the way back from these visits, Bertha would tell her daughters that the British and Americans were examining their father there, so that he could work again soon. My mother admitted to me that for years she had imagined a legal exam, only in English.

Then he came home, got his lawyer's license back, and never mentioned another word about those eighteen months. Nor about the years before that.

Inga said that in his will, Hinnerk had stated that his diary should be burned after his death. So they burned it.

"Didn't you take a look at it beforehand?" a doubting Rosmarie asked.

"No," Inga said, looking Rosmarie in the eye.

Hinnerk loved fire. He spent entire days building fires in the garden; he would stand there and poke at the blaze with a pitchfork. Whenever Rosmarie, Mira, and I joined him, he would say, "There are three things, you know, that you can never tire of looking at. The first is water, the second is fire. And the third is other people's misfortunes."

You could still see the scorch marks on the kitchen floor where the British soldiers had made their fire. But the red graffiti on the chicken shed had now vanished beneath the white paint. Well, almost. If you knew it was there you could see it. But I reckoned we had done enough. I went around the corner to see Max. He had put the large roller to one side and was now painting with the brush.

"How far have you got, then?"

Max didn't look up; he kept painting with great concentration.

"Hey, Max! It's me. Are you okay? Have you got compulsive painting disorder? Cramp? Should I help you?"

Max brushed around wildly in the center of the wall. "No, I'm fine."

I came closer, but he stood in my way and said, "Oh, have you finished your wall already? Let me have a look. Can you still make out the N-word?"

He jostled me back around to my side of the shed, took a look at it, and said, "It's come out well."

"You can still see it."

"Yes, but only if you really want to."

I stared at the white wall. "Crikey! Is this chicken shed now symbolic somehow?"

But Max wasn't listening. He had disappeared behind the shed again. It was getting dark. The painted wall was shining white. Why was he behaving so oddly? I went around and stood next to him, but still he didn't look at me. I could see that he wasn't painting the wall evenly from one side to the other but had started in the middle. No, he was painting over something. For a second I thought there must have been a second scrawl of red graffiti that I hadn't seen and that he was trying to hide from me. To protect me, maybe. But then I saw that he was painting over something he'd written himself. My name. About a dozen times.

"Iris, I . . ."

"I like the wall."

The two of us stood and looked at it for a while.

"Come on, Max, let's stop. It's too dark to paint now."

"You go on in. I'm just going to finish this."

"Don't be daft."

"No, really, I'm enjoying it. Anyway, it was my idea to start painting tonight."

As you wish, I thought. I turned around and started clearing up my painting things.

"Leave all that. I'll do it. I will."

I shrugged and wandered slowly through the garden to the front door. When I passed the roses I noticed how their scent was more powerful in the evening than during the day.

I drank a large mug of hot milk and took Hinnerk's book of poetry with me to bed. It was written in old-fashioned

German script, but then again I was a librarian. All the same, I had to get used to his handwriting. The first poem was an eight-line verse about fat and thin women. Then there was a long one about farmers who exposed crafty lawyers while pretending to play dumb. There was a rhyming formula for preventing the plague, which began:

> *Lungwort, butterbur, speedwell too,*
> *Angelica and sea cole,*
> *Juniper, gentian white not blue,*
> *Birthwort swallowed whole . . .*

I read poems about will-o'-the-wisps on the fen, an old harbor on the Geeste that had silted up long ago and where an empty barque would anchor at full moon in September—and whenever it anchored, a child from the village would be missing the following day. Hinnerk wrote about the rich sound made by four men swinging their flails, threshing in the fields. There was a poem about emigrants to America. One was entitled "August 24th," and described the day the storks depart. Another told of an ice harvest at the pond outside the village. I read a slightly crude verse about the parish copper who injured a cow, which then had to be slaughtered. Yet another was about the dance in the barn at Tietjens." And at the end there were two odd poems, one of which was called "The Twelve." It was about the six final nights of the old year and the six first ones of the new. Anybody who hung their washing out at this time would soon be wrapped in a burial shroud. Anybody who turned a wheel, even a spinning wheel, would soon be driven in a hearse. Because in this period the great deer hunter charges through the air. The final poem in the gray book was about the massive fire in Bootshaven the year before Hinnerk was born. In it the people scream like cattle and the cattle scream like people as half the village is consumed by fire.

I switched off the lamp on the bedside table and stared into the blackness of the room. After my eyes had become used to it I could make out shadows and outlines. There wasn't a single poem in Hinnerk's gray book about the war. Nor were there any that suggested they had been written in a camp. In a camp whose purpose was to make the inmates recall gruesome deeds from recent years: their own and those of others. I thought of the poems that dealt with Hinnerk's village and were imbued with love for the places of his childhood. His childhood that he had hated so much.

And I realized that not only was forgetting a form of remembering, but remembering was a form of forgetting, too.

Chapter IX

OF COURSE I THOUGHT ABOUT MAX. I thought about whether he was holding back because I was holding back and whether I was holding back because he was holding back or because I wanted to hold myself back for reasons I had to think about.

The following morning, it must have been Tuesday, I went barefoot to the large wardrobe and opened the doors. It smelled of wool, wood, and camphor, with a trace of my grandfather's hair tonic. After a short deliberation I pulled out a white dress with light gray polka dots that had once been Inga's ball gown. It was thin and light: perfect, for it seemed as if the heat wave was going to last. I sat on the steps by the front door with a cup of tea and breathed in the confident fragrance of summer. I saw the three empty paint pots at the bottom of the steps only when I was about to go back inside. I walked along the side of the house to the copse. And there it was: all four walls of the chicken shed were now painted white. It was what I had feared. It looked glorious, like a little summerhouse. How long had Max gone on painting yesterday? As I circled it, I could still see the word "Nazi" grinning through the white paint. The multiple "Irises" were no longer visible though. I went into the tiny house, but had to duck my head to stand up inside.

Whenever we were caught off guard by the rain, Rosmarie, Mira, and I would shelter in here. But I was often here on my own, too. Especially later on when I came to visit during the holidays. Sometimes Rosmarie would already be back at school in September, but not me. I would have the mornings to myself. I collected stones that looked completely different from the ones back home. We mainly had smooth, round pebbles, but here there were stones that looked, and almost broke, like glass. If you threw them against a patch of hard ground, pieces would splinter off, as sharp as knife blades. "Flint stones," Mira called them. Most of them were light brown, gray brown, or black; only the odd one was white.

The Rhine pebbles that we had back home didn't splinter. For a time I broke open lots of them in the hope of finding crystals inside. I had a good eye for these stones; the rougher and plainer they were on the outside, the more they sparkled inside. I would find them mostly on the old railway tracks that ran through the forest near our house. I could tell by their form whether there was anything inside worth finding. There was something in their roundness that seemed less arbitrary than that of normal stones. Sometimes the crystals would be visible on the surface, like glass windows you could look through. My father gave me a stonecutting saw and I would spend hours in our cellar sawing through stones. The blade made a horrible noise that hurt my ears. I would look eagerly into the glittering cavities. Although I felt triumph and pride when my assumptions were proved correct, I also knew that I was breaking into something forbidden, destroying secrets. And yet I was relieved that the brown stones weren't just stones but crystal caves for fairies and tiny magical beings.

Later, I moved on to collecting words and mining the crystalline realms of hermetic poetry. But behind all this collecting was the same craving for magical, animated worlds in sleeping things. When I was a child I had a vocabulary book where I kept special words, in the same way that I would collect mussels and special stones. They were listed under the following categories: "beautiful words," "ugly words," "false words," "contorted words," and "secret words." Under "beautiful words" I had written: *rosy, fragrant, pitter-patter, banana, mellifluous, foxglove, lullaby*. The "ugly words" were: *scrotum, gurnard, moist, crabby*. "False words" angered me because they pretended to be harmless but in fact they were nasty or dangerous, like "aftershock" and "growth." Or they pretended to be magical, like "mangold" and "kingpin," but were disappointingly normal. Or they described something that wasn't clear to anybody: no two people would picture the same color if they heard the word "crimson."

The "contorted words" were a sort of hobby of mine—
or perhaps an illness. Maybe it amounted to the same thing.
My favorite animals included the "hippotatomus," the
"rhinosheros" and the "woodspeckler." I found it funny to
"hoover over the abyss," and loved the line from *Richard III*
that went: "Now is the discount of our winter tents." I knew
what "antidisestablishmentarianism" was, but what was
"pantyfishersentscaryrhythm"? I fancied it could be a men-
acing drumbeat to which one might retrieve one's knickers
from the lake.

The "secret words" were the hardest to find, but that
was not surprising. They were words that behaved as if they
were entirely normal but in fact harbored something quite
different, something wonderful. So the opposite of the
"false words." I was comforted by the fact that the sports
stadium at our school was home to a sweet-sounding holy
man. His name was St. Adium and he was the patron saint of
word games.

Or road signs warning of a "Hidden Dip." These were
actually saying that if you looked hard enough on the road-
side you might come across a delicious tub of taramasalata,
hummus, or tzatziki. Every time we passed such a sign I
would imagine taramasalata spread thickly on toasted white
bread with a squeeze of lemon juice and freshly ground
black pepper. Or that very rare but delicious fish, the perch-
ance, dusted in seasoned flour then fried. Absolute heaven.

My recollections had made me hungry so I went inside.
There was practically nothing left to eat in the kitchen;
I munched on some black bread and nut chocolate, and
decided to go shopping later.

I ran upstairs and fetched a towel from the small washing basket in Inga's room. It had a flowery pattern but was as stiff as a board. I fastened it to the pannier rack and rode to the lake. It was a normal working day; I had a guilty conscience because I wasn't in the library, nor was I sorting out my inheritance. I wasn't even shattered by grief. Well, I reminded myself, I had taken some time off, even if only via an answerphone. I hadn't left an address or telephone number, but so what? I would have to try to get hold of my boss again later.

My work, of course, was nothing more than me continuing to collect secrets. And just as I had stopped sawing into stones I suspected might contain crystals, I had also stopped reading books that interested me and started getting interested in books that nobody read anymore.

When we were younger, Rosmarie always made fun of the fact that I took it personally if the nuts we cracked open were empty. I couldn't stop wondering how the nut had escaped from its closed shell. Her favorite trick was to spoon out a soft-boiled egg and hand it over to me at breakfast with the hole hidden in an egg cup. I would howl each time I cracked open the shell and put my spoon into the void. And now this house had been handed over to me. If I declined, I would dream about it forever.

An early-morning mist hung over the lake. I laid my bike on the grassy slope and undressed. My dress floated down to the dew like a cloud. I spread out my towel and put my things on it to stop them from getting drenched. When I waded into the water tiny fish scattered from around my ankles, darting into the safety of the dark. It was cold. Once more I wondered about all the things that were swimming around in here. I had never been taken by the idea of scuba diving; angry seas, sad gravel pits, and dark bog lakes suited me, because in the end I didn't want to know exactly.

I swam across the lake with long strokes. Small air bubbles tickled my stomach. Swimming naked was wonderful; I could feel resistance and turbulence over the entire surface of my body. Let's face it, you don't exactly become more streamlined without a swimming costume on. But at least these days I had a body that I regarded as my own. It had taken long enough. Devouring books and bread had made my mind light and my body sluggish. Because I never liked looking at myself back then, I would reflect myself in stories. Eat, read, read, eat. When, later on, I stopped reading, I also stopped bingeing. I remembered my body again. I had one now. A bit neglected, maybe, but it was there and I was surprised by its diversity of forms, lines, and surfaces. The communal changing room at the swimming pool would no longer be my downfall; I knew it was time for the individual ladies' cabins.

Downfall, windfall, fallacies, falling, Rosmarie for remembrance. Her body fell to ruin before it was even all there. All young girls are obsessed by their bodies because they don't have bodies yet. They are like nymphs that live underwater for years, eating and eating. Every so often they acquire a new skin and they keep on eating. Then the nymphs climb out of the water on a long stalk, shed their skin a final time, and fly off as dragonflies. She might have managed it. When Harriet was Rosmarie's age she was already able to fly.

*

A few meters before reaching the far bank I turned around and swam back. By now the mist had almost disappeared; there was only a thin layer above the surface of the water. I was just able to touch the ground with my feet when I saw Max. After laying his bike beside mine he didn't look over at me, just ripped off his shirt and shorts and ran into the water with a splash. He dived in and began swimming the crawl straightaway. But as he was about to pass me, he stopped, turned to me, and raised his hand.

"Hi, Iris!"

"Good morning."

He came closer. I didn't know what to say. Clearly he didn't, either. We stood facing each other but averted our eyes. I used the water like a blanket, pulling it up to my chin; I glanced at his shoulder and watched the drops running off it. Although I couldn't see where he was looking, so close to me, I could feel it. Quickly, I crossed my arms over my breasts. Then, finally, his eyes met mine.

He slowly took his hand out of the water and traced the line of my shoulder with his forefinger. His hand disappeared back into the water. He was standing quite close; I pressed my arms more tightly to my body. He leaned forward and kissed me on the lips. He felt warm and soft and good. I must have made a grab for his shoulders. I was light-headed. Max pulled me toward him. When my breasts touched his chest I could feel his body tighten. What I did after that I can't say with any certainty, nor how long I did it for. But soon afterward we ended up on the narrow patch of sand at the shore. I could feel the coolness of the water on his body beneath me, his penis inside his wet trunks, his lips on my neck. As I was helping him take off his trunks he suddenly held me firmly in his arms.

"I don't have sex outdoors with clients."

"Really? Haven't you noticed that this is precisely what you're doing now?"

"Oh God! I don't have sex with clients full stop. Not outdoors or anywhere else."

"Are you sure?"

"No. Yes! No. Iris, what are you doing to me?"

"Sex outdoors?"

"Iris. You're driving me crazy. Your smell, your walk, your lips and the way you speak."

"My what?"

I rolled off him and onto the sand. Max was probably right. It was a stupid idea: he was Mira's little brother. Not only that, he was my lawyer and my aunts' lawyer; we still had to discuss what was going to happen to the house if I didn't take it. What we were doing right now would only complicate matters unnecessarily. My relationship with his sister and Rosmarie had also been complicated. He had no idea just how complicated. I covered my eyes with my hands. Beneath my forefinger I could feel the scar on the bridge of my nose.

Then I felt his fingers on my hands.

"Come here, Iris. What's wrong? Hey!" Max's voice was soft and warm, just like his mouth. "Iris, you can't begin to imagine how much I'd love to sleep with you. I don't even dare tell you that I'd even like to sleep with you in the chicken shed, in your bed, in my bathroom, in the DIY store, and, God forgive me, in the cemetery."

I couldn't help smiling beneath my hands. "Oh really?"

"Yes!"

"In the DIY store?"

"Yes!"

"So, with white paint running down between my breasts?"

"No. That's the chicken-shed fantasy. In the DIY store I saw all these screws and nuts and drills and rawlplugs and . . ."

I sat up and saw that Max was trying to stop himself from laughing. The very effort of it was making him wince. When he saw me looking at him he burst out laughing. I punched him in the chest; he fell onto his back, laughing all the while. He had grabbed hold of my arms and pulled me down with him so that my naked torso was lying on his once more. It was like a power surge. Now he wasn't laughing anymore.

I could have had sex with him there and then. Instead he pushed me away, somewhat roughly, shook his head, and dived back into the lake. Without looking around he swam off. I stood up, pulled on my dress, and rode away.

I stood the bicycle by the front door, went inside, and changed into my black funeral clothes—a smart move, I thought, after my experience with the golden dress at the DIY store. I picked up my bag and rode to the Edeka shop. I bought bread, milk, butter, almonds, two types of cheese, carrots, tomatoes, more nut chocolate, and, because I felt so hot, some watermelon. Back home I put everything in the fridge, rang Freiburg, and spoke to my boss. Again she offered her condolences and said she appreciated that I still had to sort out my inheritance.

"Do it as quickly as you can," she said with a sigh. "The

sooner these things are resolved, the better. My brother and I still haven't come to an agreement even though our parents have been dead for years. Yes, it's very busy here. The vacation is almost upon us but don't worry, we've got enough staff. Frau Gerhard is back from her break. So stay as long as is necessary. You don't sound terribly well, Frau Berger. I see. So I shouldn't expect you here this week? Yes. That's fine. I understand. Good-bye, good-bye, ciao, Frau Berger."

I hung up. I didn't sound terribly well? Obviously not. I was upset, confused, and hurt by Max's rejection. But how did I react? I withdrew coyly. I realized with disdain that I hadn't come much further than the women of the previous generation, with regard to being in control of one's life. But that was no surprise. I mean, I was the product of the most uptight of the three Lünschen sisters.

Christa was attached to Bootshaven, to large skies above empty spaces, to the wind in her brown hair that she still wore short. When she read or heard Storm's poem about the gray city "by the gray sea" her eyes would water and she would recite the third verse in a trembling voice that I didn't like. When, as a child, and later as a teenager, I came into the living room on certain summer evenings, I might find my mother sitting there in the twilight. She would be perched on the edge of the sofa, her hands beneath her thighs, rocking back and forth. Her eyes fixed on the floor. She didn't rock dreamily, but made short, jerky movements. Parts of her body seemed to be fighting against others. Her pointed boy's knees kept digging into her breasts. Her teeth clamped her lower lip. Her thighs squashed her hands.

My mother would never normally sit around like this.

Either she would be busy in the garden, weeding, pruning, harvesting berries, hacking, mowing, digging, or planting. Or she would be hanging up washing, filling or clearing out shelves and boxes, pressing sheets, duvet covers, and towels with the mangle in the basement. She baked cakes or made jam. Or she wasn't there at all because she was jogging through the dusty asparagus fields, on a "forest run" as she used to call it. When Christa sat down on the sofa in the evenings it was only to watch the television news or read the paper and doze off soon afterward. At some point she would wake with a start, confused, and grumble at us. It was late and high time that we—my father and I—went to bed; she, Christa, was going up at any rate. Which was what she did.

But on those rare evenings that I found her on the sofa—there may have been seven or eight of them altogether—she had turned up the record player loud. Unusually loud. Unsuitably loud. Rebelliously loud. I knew the record. On the sleeve was a picture of a man with a beard, a fisherman's smock, and a captain's hat, in a meadow somewhere or on a beach, singing songs in Low German to the guitar. "*Ick wull wi weern noch kleen, Jehann!*" he boomed out to all four corners of our living room, his song more a challenge than a lament. I didn't know whether I should leave, because it was quite clear that I was intruding. But I didn't leave, for I wanted it to stop. I wanted my mother to become my mother again, and not Christa Lünschen, the ice-skater from Bootshaven. It broke my heart to see her sitting there, rocking back and forth, and I blamed myself, because obviously my father and I didn't make her happy. But I was also disgusted; for me her homesickness was a betrayal.

So I stayed by the door, unable to go in to her but unable to leave, either. If it went on for too long I started fidgeting. My mother would look up in fright; sometimes she would even scream. She jumped to her feet and snatched off the record. In a voice that was supposed to sound cheerful she said, "Iris! I didn't hear you there at all! How was Anni's?"

It sounded clearly as if she had been caught in the act, which meant she must have something to hide. So it *was* betrayal. I said, scornfully, "What on earth were you listening to? Terrible."

Then I went into the living room, opened the cupboard where the sweets were—which I was allowed to do only if I had asked permission—broke off a large chunk of chocolate, turned around, and went up to my room to read.

Had Bertha felt homesick, too? Bertha, who had always lived in her house. The fact that a care home was called a home was a disgrace that ensured that "home" would always top the list of "false words."

After Bertha had been taken from her house to a home, she no longer knew where she was. And yet she seemed to know where she wasn't. She was forever stuffing cases, bags, plastic bags, coat pockets full of things. And she asked anybody who came near her, visitors, nurses, or fellow residents, whether they could take her home. The care home upset Bertha. It was an expensive private home. But the patients with dementia were undoubtedly at the bottom of the pecking order. Health was the most prized commodity. The fact that someone may have once been a mayor, a rich society lady, or a renowned scientist was irrelevant. On the contrary, the higher someone's former standing, the further they had to fall. People in wheelchairs might be able to play bridge, but they couldn't go to tea dances. It was an incontrovertible fact.

Apart from a clear mind and physical health there was one other thing that could win you respect and status in the home: visitors. What counted here was the frequency of the visits, how regular they were and how long they lasted. It also helped if it wasn't always the same people who came. Men counted more than women. Younger visitors were better than older ones. Residents of the home whose families came often were respected: they must have done something in their lives to deserve it.

Bertha's most loyal friend from her social circle, Thede Gottfried, had come every second Tuesday morning—her sister-in-law was at the same care home. Christa only visited Bertha during school holidays, but then she came every day. Aunt Harriet came every weekday, Aunt Inga every weekend.

Bertha forgot her daughters one by one. The eldest first. Although she remembered for a long time that Christa belonged to her, the name meant nothing. First she called her Inga, then Harriet. Inga was still Inga for a while, then she became Harriet, too. Harriet remained Harriet for ages, but one day, much later, even Harriet was a stranger.

"Like the three little pigs," Rosmarie said.

I didn't know what she meant.

"You know, the first one's house is blown down so it runs into the second one's house; that's blown down, too, so the both of them run into the third one's house."

Bertha's house of stone. Was it now going to be mine?

At the time my mother took it very badly that her mother couldn't remember her name. Maybe she felt it was unfair that she was unable to forget her home but her home could so easily forget her. Inga and Harriet were more relaxed about the matter. Inga held Bertha's hand and stroked it and looked into Bertha's eyes with a smile. Bertha liked that. Harriet took Bertha to the loo, wiped her, washed her hands. And Bertha told Harriet how kind she was and how glad she was to have her.

Inga didn't care that she was called Harriet, but when Bertha once called her Christa she got annoyed. Christa wasn't there. She didn't hold Bertha's hand. She didn't go to the loo with Bertha. She had a husband. Hinnerk had loved her the most. Some things could never be forgiven. When Christa was there during school holidays and looked after Bertha, it was hard for Inga and Harriet to be civil to her and fair-minded. When Christa was sad and shocked by the deterioration of Bertha's memory, her younger sisters found it hard to feel compassion. They felt contempt instead. Their sister had no idea how bad, strenuous, and frightening it really was.

Last Sunday, early in the afternoon, Bertha finally died of a summer flu. Her body had simply forgotten how to recover from an illness like that.

Aunt Inga held her hand. She called for a nurse. Then she phoned Harriet, who drove to the home at once, just in time to see her mother draw her final breath. Bertha's eyebrows were pinched together slightly, as if she were trying to think of something. Her long and pointed nose stuck out from her face. A plastic beaker of apple juice stood on the white bedside table.

They didn't call Christa until the evening. My mother put down the receiver and started crying. Afterward she asked my father over and over again, "Why did they wait so long before telling me? Why? What were they thinking of? How much can they hate me?"

There are some things you can never forgive.

At the graveside, we lined up to take turns to throw our flowers onto the oak coffin. The three sisters stood close together, Christa on the right, Inga in the middle, Harriet on the left. My mother slipped her large black bag from her shoulder and opened it. It was only then that I noticed the bag was bulging. Christa took a step forward, peered into the bag, and hesitated. She pulled out something; it had red and yellow hoops. A stocking? She threw it into the open grave. Then she took out from her bag the other stocking—or was it an oven cloth?—and threw it in. Everyone was silent, all the mourners trying to work out what Christa was doing. Her sisters also stepped forward and stood beside her. Finally, with a vigorous gesture, Christa turned the bag upside down and just tipped everything out. It was then that I recognized what she was shaking into her mother's grave: the knitted things from the box in the wardrobe, the holes in Bertha's memory turned into wool.

When the bag was empty my mother snapped it shut and hung it back awkwardly over her shoulder. Inga's right hand felt for the hand of her elder sister, her left hand took Harriet's. For a while the three of them stood like that by the hole in the ground where Bertha lay at rest beneath garish knitted items. Now they were Hinnerk's "bonny lasses" again. And they knew that they would always be strongest together as a trio.

So what was the truth about Aunt Inga, the bonniest lass of the three? I wanted to know once and for all, so I put on the thin white dress that was lying on the chair. My black one was soaked in sweat again. I climbed onto the bike and rode off.

Herr Lexow lived right beside the school, which wasn't far from the church, which wasn't far from the house. Nothing here was far from anything else. I didn't know if I would actually ring his doorbell, but as it happened he was in the garden doing a spot of weeding. He must have already watered because the pungent smell of damp, warm earth hung over the flower beds. As I got off my bike, he looked up.

"Ah, it's you." He sounded subdued but not unhappy to see me.

"Yes, it's me again. I'm really sorry to disturb you, but—"

"Please come in, Iris. You're not disturbing me at all."

I wheeled my bike through the small gate and leaned it against the side of the house. The garden was pretty and well tended: huge cosmos billowing all over the place, marguerites, roses, lavender, and poppies. He had precisely defined beds of potatoes, runner beans, and tomatoes. I could see red currant and black currant bushes, gooseberries and a hedge of raspberry canes. Herr Lexow offered me a seat on a bench in the shade of a hazel bush, went into the house, and came out again shortly afterward with a tray and two glasses. I jumped up to help. He said there was juice and water in the kitchen. I brought out the sticky bottle of homemade elder-berry juice and a bottle of mineral water. Herr Lexow filled our glasses and sat beside me on the bench. I complimented his garden and the juice, and he nodded. Then he looked at me and said, "Spit it out, then."

I laughed. "I bet you were a good teacher."

"Yes. I was. But most importantly I remained one for a long time. So?"

"I need to talk about Bertha again."

"I'd be glad to. There aren't many people I can talk to Bertha about."

"Tell me about her. Did you help her when my grandfa-ther was away? How was she with the children?" I wanted to find out more about Inga, of course, but I didn't dare ask so directly.

It was pleasantly warm on the bench in the shade. After all the excitement of the morning at the lake I now felt heavy and tired. I closed my eyes and listened to Herr Lexow's calm voice amid the humming of the bees.

There was no doubt that Bertha loved Hinnerk Lünschen, but he didn't treat her the way she deserved. She should have been more assertive with him, but in all likelihood he wouldn't have married her if she had. And she did love him. Did Hinnerk love her? Maybe. Definitely. In his own way. He loved her because she loved him and that may have been what he loved most about her: her love for him.

And Inga. A beautiful girl. Herr Lexow would have loved to have been her father, but ultimately he didn't know if she was his. She may well have been, but he never spoke to Bertha about it. He didn't dare, and he always thought it was a conversation that they could have when they were old, when Hinnerk was dead, when worldly things didn't matter anymore, but that stage never came. And then it was too late. There came a time when Bertha didn't want to talk to him anymore. She would gladly say hello but wouldn't answer any questions. She said, "That was all so long ago." And this hurt Herr Lexow. Only later did he understand that she evaded questions simply because she could no longer answer them.

Inga was born during the war, December 1941, when Hinnerk was still at home. Earlier that year, during the Easter holidays, Herr Lexow had taken the time to bring Bertha a few dahlia tubers. She had admired these flowers the previous autumn, they were absolutely stunning: powerful claret stems and thick lavender-colored blooms, a most unusual color for dahlias. Herr Lexow had never forgotten that night in the Deelwaters' garden, just as he could never forget Bertha's sister, Anna. He brought the basket of tubers into the kitchen. He had come in the back way through the barn; that was what you did in the village—only strangers rang the doorbell. Bertha was shelling prawns. She was wearing a blue apron, there was a bowl of prawns on the table and some newspaper on her lap that she dropped the shells into. Herr Lexow put his woodchip basket by the door to the cellar. The tubers could go into the ground the following week or the one after that. They talked about Anna. He wanted to know whether Anna had talked to Bertha shortly before she died. Bertha looked at him thoughtfully, without interrupting her shelling. Her fingers took the prawns; she snapped them with her thumb just behind the head and pulled the two halves of the shell apart—quickly, firmly, but delicately so that the legs and black spinal cord came away. Bertha said nothing and bent over the prawns again. He looked at her; a strand of blond hair had come loose from her updo. Before he could think about what he was doing he took the hair and swept it behind her ear. Startled, she reached for her hair and her hand met his. Bertha's hand was cold and smelled of the sea. Yes, she whispered. Yes, Anna did talk. But she hadn't really understood what she said. But yes, it did have something to do with him, Herr Lexow.

Carsten Lexow's mind was in a spin. That night was now fifteen years ago. Since then he had thought about her every single day. He dropped to his knees in front of Bertha and stammered something; she looked at him, at a loss but full of sympathy, and took his head between her wrists. Tiny pink feelers and legs stuck to her wet prawn fingers. The newspaper with the shells slipped from Bertha's legs. He buried his face in her lap; his body shuddered, whether from crying or something else Bertha couldn't tell. With the underside of her forearm she stroked his back as if he were a child.

Little Christa was not at home. The housemaid, Agnes, had gone to see her mother, who had sprained her ankle. Agnes had to look after her, but had taken Christa with her so that her mother's accident did not inconvenience Bertha. Hinnerk was at work, not at the office but with prisoners. Herr Lexow calmed down but left his head where it was. He took hold of Bertha's legs and began stroking them from the ankles upward, under her skirt. He put his face into the apron and breathed in the fishy smell. Bertha was no longer thinking that he was like a little child. She became very still and held her breath. Snippets of sentences, words of love, agitated sobs drifted into her ears and she let him go on. She just sat there, silently, frowning and feeling her belly getting warmer and heavier. And although she loved Hinnerk rather than Herr Lexow, she hadn't felt a sensation like this in five years of marriage. Carsten Lexow kneeled up and kissed her, and knew that it wasn't the same mouth from that night. He was about to leave when he saw tears streaming down her cheeks. Not just one or two, but lots of them, a deluge. Her apron was already soaked across her breasts, but her shoulders weren't moving, nor did she make any sound. Her neck was red and wet and salty when he kissed it.

She stood up abruptly, wiped her hands clean on the apron, and went into the bedroom opposite the kitchen. She drew the green curtains and untied her apron. She removed her shoes, her skirt and blouse, and got into bed. Carsten Lexow took off his trousers, shirt, and socks and placed everything neatly on the floor by the bed. He went to her and took her in his arms while thinking of that night in the garden. Back then, had he loved the wrong one and kissed the right one? Or loved the right one and kissed the wrong one? Was there not perhaps the hint of a taste of apples there among the fish and salt?

And yet, all the while that Carsten Lexow was in Bertha's bed, tears streamed down her cheeks like two inlets.

That same night she made love with her husband, too, who had been given black bread topped with prawns and a fried egg for dinner. The muddy dahlia tubers still stood in the kitchen, shining yellow in the dim light. She said that Herr Lexow had popped over with the basket.

"He has a good life, that Herr Lexow. Holidays, flowers. In the middle of a war, too." Hinnerk snorted his contempt, hacked off a piece of bread and forked it into his mouth. Bertha watched some of the delicate pink prawns fall back onto the plate.

Nine months later, Inga came into the world. On that night there was one of those rare, eerie winter storms where hailstones the size of cherries rain down and lightning flashes through the sky. Frau Koop, who was with Bertha during her labor, swore that lightning struck the house and shot into the earth via the lightning conductor.

"And if we'd put that baby girl in the bath she'd be dead now."

She usually added, "But the littl 'un definitely got something from it, poor lass."

If Rosmarie was there she would ask in a higher voice than usual, "Poor little worm, wasn't it?"

Frau Koop would cast her a suspicious look, but wouldn't know what to say, so she would fall into an eloquent silence.

Herr Lexow had stopped talking. He was looking at me expectantly. My daydream faded and I sat up somewhat dizzily.

"I'm sorry, what did you say?"

"I asked whether she'd ever spoken about me."

"Who are we talking about now?"

"Bertha."

"No, Herr Lexow, I'm sorry. Not to me. Not even later on. Well . . ."

"Well?"

"Once, twice maybe. But no, I don't know. Once or twice she said, 'The teacher's here,' if someone came in. But I can't recall any more than that."

Herr Lexow nodded. And looked at the floor.

I stood up. "Thank you, I really appreciate you having told me all of this."

"Well, there wasn't that much. But it was my pleasure. Please send my regards to your mother and aunts."

"Oh please, don't get up. I'm just going to wheel my bike out and I'll close the gate behind me."

"That's Hinnerk Lünschen's bicycle."

"You're right. It is his. It still rides excellently."

Herr Lexow gave a nod to the bike and closed his eyes.

Chapter X

I CYCLED BACK TO THE HOUSE. I had to get clear in my mind what was going to happen to my inheritance. Perhaps I ought to have paid closer attention to what Herr Lexow was saying rather than dozing in his garden. But who was to say that his story was any truer than my daydreams? After all, Aunt Inga had always been a woman full of mystery. Legends suited her.

How true were the stories people told me, and how true were those that I stitched together myself from memories, guesswork, fantasies, and eavesdropping? Sometimes fabricated stories became true in hindsight, and some stories fabricated the truth. Truth is closely related to forgetting; I knew this because I still read dictionaries, encyclopedias, catalogs, and other reference books. In the Greek word for truth, *aletheia*, the underworld river Lethe flows covertly. Whoever drank from this river discarded their memories as they already had their mortal coil, in preparation for the realm of shadows. And so the truth was what was not forgotten. But did it make sense to look for the truth where there was no forgetting? Didn't truth prefer to hide in the cracks and holes of memory? I couldn't get any further with words.

Bertha could put a name to all plants. When I thought of my grandmother I pictured her in the garden, a tall figure with spindly legs and broad hips. Her slender feet would usually be wearing smart shoes. Not because she was desperately vain, but because when she came back from the village, from town, or from a friend's, she always went into the garden first rather than into the house. She wore aprons that had to be tied at the back, only seldom those that buttoned up at the front. She had a wide mouth with narrow, faintly curved lips. Her long, pointed nose was a little red and her slightly prominent eyes were often wet with tears. She had blue eyes. Forget-me-not blue.

Bertha would walk between the beds with a slight stoop, her gaze focused on the plants. Sometimes she would bend down to pick out a weed, but generally she was accompanied by her garden hoe as if it were a shepherd's crook. A sort of iron stirrup was fixed to the end of the handle. She would dig it into the earth and shake the handle forcefully with both hands. It looked as if it was the hoe waggling her rather than the other way around. As if she had cut into an electric cable by mistake. But the only things buzzing were the metallic blue dragonflies in the shimmering air.

The center of the garden was where it was hottest; nothing cast its shadow there. Bertha barely seemed to notice this. Only very rarely would she stop what she was doing and, with an unconscious, graceful movement of her hand, stroke her damp hair from the nape of her neck back up into her bun.

The more that was cut from her memory, the more they cut off her hair. But until her death, Bertha's hands still moved like those of a woman with long hair.

One day my grandmother began wandering through the garden at night. That was when she started forgetting time. She could still make out what time it was from the clock, but time meant nothing to her anymore. In summer she would put on three vests, one over the other, and woolly socks, and then she would be outraged because she was sweating profusely. She was still putting socks on her feet then. At around the same time she lost the distinction between day and night. She would get up in the night and wander around. When Hinnerk was still alive she would wander around the house at night. She did it back then because she couldn't sleep. Later, however, she roamed around outside because it would never have occurred to her that she should have been sleeping.

Harriet usually noticed when Bertha went off at night, but not always. As soon as she got wind of it she would get up with a groan, throw on her dressing gown, slip on her clogs, which were standing ready by the bed, and go outside. On those nights, Harriet thought she wouldn't be able to go on like this for long. She had a career. She had an adolescent child. By following the trail of open doors Harriet could work out which route Bertha had taken. Mostly she went out the back way, through the barn door, onto the drive and into the garden. Sometimes Harriet found her mother watering the flower beds, usually with the old tin mug in which she used to keep dried marigold seeds. Sometimes Bertha kneeled between the beds, weeding, but most of all she loved to pick flowers. She didn't pick the flower at the stem, but only the flower itself. With big umbels she would rip off the petals, which she would hold in her hand until it was too full to close. When Harriet went over to her mother, Bertha would stretch out her hand with the squashed flowers and petals and ask where she could put them. Over four cold, early-spring nights, Bertha managed to tear off the flowers from an entire bed of blue-and-white pansies. The palms of her large hands hand were stained violet for weeks afterward. As a young girl she had deadheaded the faded rose blooms with her sister, Anna, so that they flowered again rather than forming rosehips. Bertha no longer knew how old she was. She was as old as she felt, and that could mean eight, as when she called Harriet Anna, or thirty, when she talked about her husband and asked us whether he had left the office yet. People who forget time stop aging. Forgetting defeats time, the enemy of memory. For, after all, time can only heal all wounds by allying itself with forgetting.

I stood at the garden fence and fingered the scar on my forehead. I needed to think of other wounds. For years I had refused to do it. The wounds came with the house; they were part of my inheritance. And I had to take at least one look at them before I could stick the plaster of time back over them.

A long piece of sticky tape kept our hands tied behind our backs when we played the game that Rosmarie had invented and that we called Eat or Die. We played it in the garden, in the far corner where we couldn't be seen from the house, between the white currant bushes and the bramble thicket. That was also where the large compost heap was; in fact there were two of them, one a mound of earth, the other of peelings, yellowed cabbage leaves, and brown grass cuttings. The hairy leaves and fleshy stalks of pumpkins, cucumbers, and zucchini snaked their way across the ground. Bertha had planted zucchini in the garden because she loved trying out new plants, and she was delighted by the speed at which they grew. She was unsure, however, about what to do with the gigantic gourds. When she cooked them they quickly disintegrated and they didn't taste at all nice raw. So they grew and grew, and by summer the back of the garden looked like an abandoned battlefield from an earlier age, when powerful tree giants had fought each other and then left their chunky green clubs lying around.

Mint and lemon balm grew rampant here, and when our bare legs brushed against them they gave off their fresh aroma, as if they were trying to mask the foul smells from this part of the garden. Camomile grew here, too, but so did stinging nettles, ground elder, thistles, and tetterwort, which ruined our clothes with its thick yellow blood if we sat on it.

One of the three of us would be bound and blindfolded. Mostly we used Hinnerk's white silk scarf, which had a small burn mark at one end and so had been banished to the large wardrobe. We always took turns. I was usually first as I was the youngest. I would kneel down, blindfolded, my hands tied together loosely. I couldn't see a thing, but the pungent smell of the ground elder squashed beneath me mingled with the damp, warm haze of the compost heap. In early afternoon it was quiet in the garden. Flies hummed. Not the dozy black ones from the kitchen but the blue-and-green ones that always sat around cows' eyes where they drank themselves into a stupor. I could hear Rosmarie and Mira whispering; they had moved a fair distance from me. The rustling of their dresses came closer. They stood before me and one of the two girls said, "Eat or die!" Then I had to open my mouth and whoever had spoken put something on my tongue. Something they'd just found in the garden. Quickly, before I could taste anything, I would position it between my teeth, which also meant I could now determine how big it was, whether it was hard or soft, sandy or clean, and usually I could already work out what it was: a berry, a radish, a bunch of curly parsley. Only then would I put it back on my tongue, bite it, and swallow. As soon as I showed the others my empty mouth they would rip the sticky tape from my wrists. I would take the scarf from my eyes and we would laugh. Then it was the next person's turn; she would have her hands tied and eyes blindfolded.

It was astonishing just how unsettling it was if you didn't know what you were eating, or if you were expecting something different from what you got. Currants, for example, were easy to recognize. But on one occasion I thought I was holding a currant between my teeth only to find myself chewing on a fresh pea. I was distraught and disgusted. I liked peas and I liked currants, but in my mind that pea was a currant, and as a currant it was an abomination. I gagged, but I swallowed. Because if you spat it out you had to go again. And doing it again was a punishment. Whoever spat a second time was out of the game. To loud jeering she would be banished from the garden and banned from playing with the others for the rest of the day, and usually for the next day, too. Rosmarie almost never spat anything out, while Mira and I did it roughly as often as each other. Mira maybe even spat slightly more often than me, but later on I suspected that the two of them had gone somewhat easy on me. They were probably worried that I might snitch on them to my mother or Aunt Harriet.

The game would begin harmlessly and then escalate from round to round. There were afternoons when we would finish by eating earthworms, ant eggs, and rotten onions. Once I was convinced that the tiny, hairy gooseberry between my teeth—a punishment for a slippery piece of leek that I had dropped from my mouth—had to be a spider. When it burst and the juice ran over my tongue, I spat it out and it dribbled down my chin. I was out, obviously.

Another time Rosmarie was chewing a wood louse without grimacing. After she had swallowed it and her hands were free again, she carefully removed the blindfold. We held our breath. She looked at Mira and me with a glint in her eye and asked, thoughtfully, "So how many calories *are* there in a wood louse?" Then she threw her head back and laughed.

We assured her that the game was over and she had won, because we were afraid of what she might do as payback.

We also played the game on the day before Rosmarie's death. It had been raining nonstop for two days, but in the afternoon the sun broke through the clouds. Mira walked slowly down the drive toward the house; we hadn't seen her for the past two days. She leaned her back against one of the lime trees. She yawned and turned her face to the sun. With her eyes closed she said, "We're going to play Eat or Die."

It was usually Rosmarie who determined what we played, but she just shrugged and pushed back her long red hair with the backs of her hands. "I'd rather go to the lock, but I don't mind. Why not?"

I would rather have gone to the lock, too. We had been stuck inside for so long that I would have loved a race across the pasture. But I was more delighted by the fact that Rosmarie hadn't decided what we were doing this time, so I said, "Yes, let's play what Mira wants."

Rosmarie shrugged her shoulders again, turned around, and went into the garden. She was wearing the golden dress and it glistened in the sun when she moved. I walked behind her. Mira followed us at a distance. The garden was steaming. Large rainwater lenses sat on the cucumber and pumpkin leaves through which you could see the veins and hairs magnified. Behind the currant bushes it smelled of earth and cat poo.

"Have you got the blindfold and the tape?"

Rosmarie had turned around and was staring at Mira and me with her pale eyes. Mira stared back; there was something challenging in her gaze that I didn't understand. She had more mascara on than usual and her eyeliner was particularly bold. The dark makeup clung thickly and heavily to the curved lashes. When she moved her eyes it looked as if two black caterpillars were crawling across her face.

"No, we haven't." On that day Mira's face was like ash, as was her voice. Only her eyes seemed to be alive, and the black caterpillars writhed silently.

"I'll get them," I said, running indoors, up the stairs, and fetching the tape. There wasn't much left but it would be enough. I opened the large wardrobe, grabbed Hinnerk's scarf, which was hanging over a tie rack on the inside of the door, hitched up my light blue skirt, clattered down the stairs again, and went back into the garden.

Mira and Rosmarie hadn't moved from where they were; Rosmarie was talking to Mira, who was looking at the ground. But when they saw me coming they both turned away at the same time and walked off. I didn't catch up until we got to the currant bushes.

"Here are the things."

"Do you want to start, Iris?" Rosmarie asked.

"No, I'm going to start this time," Mira said.

I shrugged and gave Mira the scarf; she tied it over her eyes and crossed her wrists behind her back. I stuck a length of brown tape around Mira's wrists; when she saw I couldn't tear it off, Rosmarie came over, bent down quickly, and bit through it. Mira said nothing.

We kneeled in the mud behind the bushes. "It doesn't matter," Rosmarie said. "We'll wash our clothes before the Weird Sisters notice anything."

We would often wash our clothes in secret.

Rosmarie and I got up again and went off to find something to eat. I tore off a sorrel leaf and showed it to Rosmarie. She nodded and held up a leaf of her own: soup greens. That was what our grandmother called it, at any rate; it smelled of soup and Maggi, and if you rubbed it between your hands you couldn't get rid of the stench for days. I thought soup greens were a bit cruel for the first round, but I nodded and put some sorrel in my own mouth.

When we came back Mira was squatting on the ground, looking like a statue.

I said, "Okay, Mira, this is what you wanted. Eat or die. Mouth open. Are you going to give it to her, Rosmarie?"

Rosmarie crushed the leaf between her fingertips. Mira must have smelled it before it came close to her face. She opened her mouth, gave a loud groan, and vomited. The force of the eruption jerked her torso backward.

"Oh Christ! Mira!" I was so horrified that I didn't even think of taking off the blindfold and tape.

"It's fine. I feel better now. Rosmarie knows I don't like lovage."

I didn't know that soup greens were the same as lovage and I assumed that Rosmarie didn't, either. Rosmarie was silent. She kneeled behind Mira and put both arms around her. Her chin was resting on Mira's shoulder. She closed her eyes. Mira's eyes were still blindfolded. The air reeked of sick.

"Okay, come on, let's go to the lock."

I was sure that both of them would take up my suggestion. But Mira slowly shook her head.

"It's still my turn," she said. "That didn't count. I mean, it didn't even touch my tongue."

Then Rosmarie kissed Mira on the lips. The kiss unnerved me. I had never seen them kiss before, and what's more I thought of how Mira had just projectile vomited.

"You're crazy," I said. I felt uncomfortable there in the garden, although I didn't know whether it was because of the game or because of the kiss.

Rosmarie took Mira a few meters away and helped her sit down again. Then she went looking, but not very far. She bent down abruptly and when she stood up again I could see that she had picked a zucchini, not one of the clubs but a small one. A piece of zucchini was all right, I thought, particularly if it was small and fresh. But Rosmarie didn't break a piece off. Instead she muttered, "Eat it or forget it, sweetie."

Mira smiled and opened her mouth. Rosmarie crouched down right in front of her. She pinched off the flower and put the end, still wet from the rain, in Mira's mouth. And then she hissed, "This is your lover's cock."

Mira recoiled briefly. Then she became very calm, bit firmly on the end of the zucchini to break it off, and spat it blindly in Rosmarie's face. It hit Rosmarie on the upper lip. Then Mira said, "You lost, Rosmarie."

Mira tugged at the sticky tape, and it ripped open. She stood up, pulled the white scarf off her head, and threw it on the compost heap. Then she left. Rosmarie and I stared after her.

"Look, what's going on?" I asked.

Rosmarie turned to me, her face screwed up. She screamed, "Just leave me alone, you stupid, stupid idiot!"

"Fine!" I answered. "Anyway, I don't play with bad losers."

I only said that because I had seen how Mira's words had

upset Rosmarie. I hadn't understood them. Rosmarie came over to me in two long strides and slapped me.

"I hate you," I said to her.

"Worms can't hate."

I ran into the house.

Rosmarie didn't eat with the family that evening. And she didn't come up to our room until I was practically in bed. She acted as if nothing had happened. I was still angry with her. But I sat down beside her on the window seat and she explained the thing with Mira. And then night fell.

When I was there in the summer Rosmarie and I always slept together in the old marital bed. It was funny and creepy, and we would tell each other our dreams, chat, and giggle. Rosmarie talked about school, Mira, and boys she was in love with. She often talked about her father, a red-haired hulk from the north. A polar researcher, a pirate on the Arctic Ocean, maybe dead already, frozen, a silver-gray sky reflecting in sightless eyes, and other stories in that vein. She never spoke about her father with Harriet, and Harriet never mentioned him.

In bed Rosmarie and I would make up languages, secret languages, nighttime languages. For a while we said everything backward. To begin with it was a very slow process, but after a few days we were well practiced and could bounce a few short sentences back and forth. We turned around the names of everyone we knew. I was Siri, she was Eiramsor, and of course there was Arim. Then Rosmarie decided that the opposite of something would be the word for the thing itself, but with the letters reversed. So our word for eat, especially the way I did it on my own at home with my books, was "timov." Indeed this was the very opposite of "eat," only backward.

Once, when Rosmarie, Mira, and I were perched on the broad window seat in our bedroom, peering out at the rain, Rosmarie said, "Did you two know that I've absorbed Mira?"

Mira looked at her beneath her heavy lids. Languidly she opened her small, dark red mouth. "Oh really?"

"Yes. Mira is contained in Rosmarie. And you, Iris, only got away by a whisker, more precisely by a single 'i.' "

Mira and I were silent, trying to work it out in our heads. Rosmarie. After a while I said, "You know, there are a lot of things contained in you."

"I know." Rosmarie giggled gleefully.

"Sore," Mira said. After a pause she added, "Sore and arse."

"Mars," I said. After a pause I added, "I'm hungry."

We laughed.

In fact, there were multitudes contained inside Rosmarie. Sore and arse, rose and Mars, emir and sari, rear and rim.

There was nothing in me. Nothing at all. I was just myself. Iris. Flower and eye.

Enough. I had been staring long enough at the wounds that came with the house. From outside I went into the barn, then through the former utility room into the fireplace room. The glass sliding door squeaked as I pushed it open as hard as I could. The stone flags kept the whole room cool. In spite of the large glass doors it was dark in here, as the weeping willow stood too close to the terrace and only let light in through a green filter. I carried one of the wicker chairs outside. It was right here where the roof of the conservatory had been. Bertha's father had designed it himself. The local farmers had mockingly called the glass construction "The Palm House," because the Deelwaters' conservatory was very tall, not just some sort of minor extension with crown glass windows. Since then, however, the branches of the weeping willow had screened off the area from the street. Even inquisitive eyes couldn't see in anymore.

But before I thought any further about the conservatory I wanted to remember Peter Klaasen. My mother had told me some of the story, some of it I had found out myself, and Rosmarie regularly eavesdropped on Aunt Harriet's conversations with Aunt Inga, which were then relayed to me. Although Peter Klaasen was still quite young back then, maybe twenty-four, his hair had turned silver. He worked at the BP petrol station on the road out of the village. By then Inga was coming to the house more often. After Hinnerk died, Bertha's memory had started to deteriorate ever more rapidly. Although Harriet and Rosmarie lived there, Inga couldn't let Bertha be their responsibility alone. Christa lived too far away. She traveled up for the holidays with me, but that was only several times a year, so Inga tried to relieve Harriet of the burden on the weekends at least. Every Sunday evening she would get into her white VW Beetle and fill up at the BP petrol station before driving home to Bremen. Every Sunday evening she was still deep in thought even hours after her visit, caught up in a tangle of anxiety and sadness, but also relief at being able to return to her own life. And of guilt toward the one sister who wasn't able to do just that, and hatred for the other who simply carried on with her own life because she was married. Inga was forty at the time and unmarried, she had no children and didn't want any, either, but in her opinion Christa was making life incredibly easy for herself. Dietrich was a nice man on a good salary. She had a child and taught eight hours of sport per week at the secondary school in the neighboring village. Not because she needed to, but because she had been asked to, and she liked doing it. Inga knew, of course, that Christa would have helped out more if she had lived closer to Bootshaven, but she didn't and that wasn't fair. But on Sunday evenings, when everyone else was sad that the weekend was over, Inga would sit in her small noisy car and sing.

Petrol stations gave Inga the creeps. She preferred to be served. And every Sunday evening she was served by the same man with gray hair on top of a smooth, boyish face. Every Sunday he wished her a good week. She would thank him with an absentminded smile from her beautifully curved mouth. When after three months the young man called her by name, she looked at him properly for the first time.

"I'm sorry. Do you know my name?"

"I do. You come every Sunday and fill up at my garage. One should know one's regulars by name."

"I see, regulars. But how do you know who I am?" Inga was baffled. She didn't know how old the man was. He looked very young, but his hair made her unsure. Inga didn't know whether she should react with maternal condescension or cool detachment. When the pump attendant winked at her and laughed, Inga caught herself smiling back. The young man was only trying to be friendly and she was behaving like a prima donna. As she drove off she could see the young man with the gray hair in her rearview mirror, watching her while another customer was attempting to talk to him.

The next Sunday the young man was there again and greeted her politely, but without saying her name.

"Oh, come on! I'm a regular."

He gave her a candid smile. "Yes, Frau Lünschen, indeed you are, but I don't wish to be pushy."

"You're not. Not at all. I'm just a moody old bag."

The man said nothing. He looked her up and down. A look that lasted a little too long for Inga's liking.

"No, you're not. And you know it."

Inga laughed. "I believe that was a compliment. Many thanks."

I'm flirting with him, she thought in astonishment as she left the petrol station. I'm flirting with this strange pump attendant. She shook her head but couldn't help smiling.

On the Sundays that followed she would often talk with him, just briefly but enough to find herself smiling on the drive back. She found that she would only think about Bertha until she came to the edge of the village. And then, as time went on, she found herself starting to think about filling up with petrol while she was still having supper with Bertha, Harriet, and Rosmarie. She had discovered that, like her, he was there only on weekends. He was a mechanical engineer who had just finished his studies and had taken a temporary job at the petrol station. It belonged to one of his father's friends. He had found out Inga's name from the owner of the garage, who knew Inga's father from when he used to come and fill up his old black Mercedes. He was nice, not particularly eloquent, but confident. He looked handsome, was slightly vain, but most of all he was much too young, younger than Inga had first thought, and she would not allow herself to get to know him better. It was obvious that he was attracted to her, but Inga was used to this. It was why she never needed to develop an immediate interest in a man. But Peter Klaasen—by then she knew his name, too—was persistent without being overbearing.

On one of the last warm autumn days he asked her whether she liked smoked eel. When she nodded he said he was heading straight down to his smoking barrel; a friend had given him a bucket of fresh eels, already killed and gutted.

Inga laughed. "Interesting present."

"I repaired the engine of his outboard motorboat. He's got a few eel traps in the harbor. Do you want to come with me?"

"No!"

"Oh, come on! It's lovely down there."

"I know, I grew up around here."

"Okay then, do it just for me."

"Why should I?"

"Hmm, maybe because I couldn't imagine anything nicer."

After a pause, Inga said, "Is that so? Well then, I guess I'll have to."

Inga laughed at his whoops of joy and got into his car. Peter drove to a barn near the lock. Inga wasn't worried: she knew this area like the back of her hand, her family's pasture was just over there. Although Peter Klaasen liked to play the seducer with her, she enjoyed his cheerfulness and enthusiasm.

The rusty old barrel stood in the middle of the meadow. Peter went into the barn and returned with a black pail filled with the twisted bodies of dark eels. The dead creatures were still moving. He searched his jacket pockets, rummaging around in them with increasing urgency, then shook his head, cursed, and looked at Inga's legs. When he looked up again, his smile was at once mischievous and coy.

"Frau Lünschen, we're going to need your tights."

"What?"

"I'm not joking. I've forgotten mine. We need nylon tights."

"Do you want to smoke my tights or my legs?"

"Neither. We need them to get the eels. I'll buy you a new pair, I promise."

His smile was full of such expectancy that Inga sighed, went behind the car, and took off her fine mesh tights. "There you go. Now, if this little escapade doesn't start getting more entertaining soon, I'm walking straight back to the petrol station."

Peter Klaasen asked whether she would mind if he put his hand into one leg of the tights. Inga felt uneasy, but she nodded.

Peter's hand in Inga's flesh-colored tights no longer looked as if it belonged to his body. It moved around in the water inside the bucket like an eyeless, colorless deep-sea creature. And it had already caught the first eel. Inga bent over the pail. The dead eel twitched and Peter swiftly put a hook through it. He hung this hook on the iron rods that lay across the top of the barrel.

He pulled his hand out of Inga's tights and offered them to her. "Your turn now."

Inga stretched the tights over her hand, plunged it into the bucket, and grabbed for an eel, but it slipped from her grasp.

"Be brave."

Inga was bolder with her next grab and managed to get hold of it. She screamed when she pulled the eel out of the water. She could feel it moving. Peter Klaasen took it from her, skillfully, stuck a hook through its jaw, and hung it next to the other one. Inga laughed, slightly breathlessly. She handed one eel after another to Peter. When all the eels were hung he made a small fire in the oven below, but he didn't want roaring flames, he just needed it to glow.

Peter placed a round lid over the barrel. Then they sat in the car, laughing and drinking coffee from a thermos that Peter fished from the backseat. There was only one cup, for which he apologized. Inga said it didn't matter; she only had one pair of tights after all. Then the two of them burst out laughing again, and Inga felt young and relaxed and for a while she was able to forget her worries about Bertha. When Peter passed her the cup of coffee, the tips of their fingers touched. He got a shock, flinched, and the hot coffee splashed on Inga's hand. She pressed her lips together and shook her head when Peter wanted to take a look at her hand.

Later she took two freshly smoked eels back to Bremen.

Peter Klaasen offered to install a cassette player in Inga's car, and one Friday evening he rang at the front door in

Geestestrasse with his toolbox under his arm. He would get going with the installation right away so that Inga could listen to music on the drive back on Sunday. It was the Easter holidays, Mira and I were there, too; my mother had an errand to run in town.

Inga blushed when she opened the door to him, but quickly got over her embarrassment when she saw how embarrassed he was himself. She told herself that she was at least fifteen years older than this boy, and this helped her quickly regain her composure. She treated him warmly but patronizingly, with a touch of something like wistful self-mockery.

He was invited in and served tea and cake. Harriet chatted with him; she knew his boss, the owner of the petrol station, fairly well. Rosmarie was sitting at the table. In front of her stood a vase with a single dahlia, bright yellow with a pink picotee edge. She lifted her head and looked beyond the flower to Inga and her visitor. Her fine copper-red eyebrows were raised and she was eyeing up this young man with silver hair. As soon as her aunt Inga and Peter Klaasen exchanged their first words she sat bolt upright, alert and still, like an animal picking up a scent. Mira looked at Rosmarie from beneath her half-closed eyelids.

Harriet also noticed her daughter's attentiveness and had an idea. "Herr Klaasen, we've been looking for ages for someone to help Rosmarie with her math. Might you consider giving up one or two afternoons a week to do that?"

Peter Klaasen looked at Rosmarie; she looked back, but said nothing.

"Would you like that, Rosmarie?" he asked gently.

Rosmarie turned her gaze from him to Inga, who immediately started tidying her hair. Then Rosmarie looked at Mira and smiled her predatory smile, which was particularly effective as her canines were slightly longer than her incisors. "Why not?"

"Excellent," rejoiced Harriet, who couldn't believe that Rosmarie was being so amenable. "That's settled! I'll pay you twenty marks an hour."

Bertha, who was busy with her cake, looked up from her plate and said, "Oh. Twenty marks. That's a lot of money. You could . . . couldn't you? I mean, will . . . ? Come on, say something."

Peter obviously knew about Bertha; at any rate he didn't seem surprised but said pleasantly, "Yes, Frau Lünschen, it is a lot of money." But when his eyes met Inga's, he stopped suddenly. Inga looked away.

"Oh, good, good! Oh, Inga, he's going to do it!" Harriet was overjoyed. "Wait, Herr Klaasen, I need to fetch my diary so we can arrange a day. Rosmarie, which afternoon do you do gymnastics on? I'll be right back. One second, please. Okay?"

Harriet's voice rang out from the kitchen, which she had darted into in a mild panic to hunt for the diary. Her panic must have also been in part due to the fact that she felt awkward. After all, it wasn't every day you met younger admirers of your elder sister, let alone handsome ones who were mathematicians. We could hear Harriet scattily muttering to herself as she rifled through the drawer in the kitchen table.

"Wednesdays, Mama." Rosmarie rolled her eyes.

Harriet came back, brandishing a pocket diary. She fell

onto a chair. "Okay, you've got gymnastics on Wednesdays, my child, just so you know."

Rosmarie sighed heavily and shook her head in resignation.

"So what happens on the other days?" Harriet held the diary far away from her eyes and blinked. "Oh, it's so dark in here. I can't make out anything."

Peter Klaasen glanced at the dining table, took a step closer, picked up the vase with the dahlia and placed it next to Harriet's diary. Then he took a step back again. The thick yellow-and-pink flower hung like an old-fashioned reading lamp over Harriet's diary.

Harriet stared dumbfounded at the flower, then looked up and burst out laughing. Her eyes were gleaming as they looked from Peter Klaasen to her sister and back to Peter Klaasen. Bertha laughed, too, her eyes filling with tears.

Inga's heart tightened. She could barely look at him; just then she felt real love for the man. It scared her.

Even Mira smiled beneath her black fringe.

Rosmarie's eyes seemed to turn even brighter.

I couldn't help laughing, either. Then I examined the faces of the other women. In that moment we had all fallen for him.

"How about Fridays?" he asked politely.

Harriet gave him a warm smile, snapped the diary shut, and said, "Fridays it is then."

"Great," Inga said, standing up.

Peter stood up, too. Rosmarie stayed sitting and watched the two of them with anticipation. Mira glanced first at Inga and Peter, and then at Rosmarie, and then with a frown poured herself some coffee.

Bertha had taken off her shoe and showed it to me. She whispered, "This isn't mine."

"Yes it is, Grandma, it is your shoe. Put it back on again quickly or you'll get cold."

"It's very beautiful."

"Yes. Harriet bought you these shoes."

"But it doesn't belong to me. Is it one of yours?"

"No, Grandma, it's your shoe—put it on again."

"Harriet, look. Here. Where does this go?" She lifted up the shoe helplessly.

"Yes, Mum. Wait. I'll help you." Harriet crawled under the table and put Bertha's shoe back on. "That's great, Rosmarie. You can start next week." Harriet's voice came from below, sounding rather strained.

Mira put down her coffee cup and said, "I'll come along, too." Rosmarie looked at Mira; her eyes seemed even brighter yet.

"Why not," Harriet said, standing up. "We can share the cost. Would you like to join in, Iris?"

"No. I'm on holiday. And I'm two classes below them. I get free math lessons from my father anyhow. And more than I'd like." I rolled my eyes and mimed being sick.

"Why aren't my . . ." Bertha's voice sounded agitated. She had her shoe in her hand again, the other one this time. "Why . . . Oh please, Harriet, please! Why isn't it the same anymore? I mean. Will it ever be the same again? I don't think it will, will it?"

So Rosmarie and Mira got math tuition from Peter Klaasen on Friday afternoons. Afterward he would drive to the petrol station in his Citroën.

For a while it worked well. Peter enjoyed the lessons. Rosmarie and Mira were not at all as capricious as he had feared. When Rosmarie improved by a whole grade in her next math assignment, he was almost more pleased than Harriet. Also, when he had finished tutoring, he often had the opportunity for a brief conversation with Inga, who would have just arrived from Bremen. These exchanges were important to him. He had fallen in love with Inga. But not simply fallen in love; he wanted to marry her, have children with her, and be her husband forever. He had written Inga a letter in which all of this had been set out. We knew this from Rosmarie, who had secretly read it. She didn't let on to us how she had come by the letter. Inga refused to brood over her feelings. She thought she was too old or he too young, depending on how she felt at the time.

Rosmarie started hanging around the petrol station on weekends. They chatted. Peter was happy to. Whenever he talked to Inga's niece, he felt his love coming a little closer. Rosmarie's math kept on improving. When Peter explained something to her, she would gaze at him without blinking, which gave him the impression that she wasn't listening at all. But then she would surprise him with the accuracy of her answers. It was completely the opposite with Mira: she appeared to be concentrating hard, she would look at her book or knit her brow, but she failed to grasp what was being said. Her math marks were now poor, which they hadn't been before the extra lessons. But she insisted on continuing with the tuition.

Rosmarie wanted Peter. She wanted to have him. She told him she was in love with him. Said it right to his face, during a lesson and in front of Mira. Peter gaped at her, speechless. Rosmarie was a beautiful girl, tall and slim with long red hair. She had wide-set eyes. The irises were the color of glacial ice and were barely distinguishable from the bluish whites; her pupils alone stood out sharply. When I got upset with her I thought that she looked like a reptile. When we were getting on well she reminded me of a silver fairy. But either way, Mira and I found her breathtaking.

Peter was bewildered. The lesson ended earlier than usual. Inga hadn't arrived yet. But because he didn't want to miss her, he decided to hang around outside for a while longer. Rather than go to his car he strolled behind the house to the orchard. It was May, the blossom had fallen and the apples weren't yet showing. Peter's heart pounded when he saw Rosmarie approaching him from a distance.

I wasn't on holiday then, so all I knew was that Inga had called us in tears, wanting to speak to my mother. From the drive, Inga sobbed into the phone, she had seen Rosmarie and Peter kissing. She had done an immediate about-turn and driven back to Bremen. We didn't know whether Rosmarie was aware that Inga had arrived and seen them, but we assumed she knew perfectly well. Rosmarie must have heard Inga's car coming up the drive and stopping under the two lime trees. A VW Beetle doesn't have a quiet engine.

Nor did I know whether Rosmarie knew at the time that Mira was watching the kiss, too. At some point she must have found out because I heard it from my mother and she heard it from her sister Harriet, who had seen Mira witness the kiss. Mira had gone into the kitchen to fetch some lemonade, and Harriet was there. She had taken two glasses and headed into the barn. As she opened the door to the orchard and stepped outside, Rosmarie walked past her, only a few meters away, her gaze fixed on Peter. She must have spotted Mira out of the corner of her eye, but took no notice of her. Mira's forehead shone white beneath her black fringe as Harriet watched her from the kitchen, wondering at her pallor. Rosmarie had stepped past her like a sleepwalker, Mira whispered more to herself than to Harriet when she went back into the kitchen. And she hadn't dared call out to her. And just when she was about to call out to her after all, Rosmarie was already in the arms of the gray-haired pump attendant. Beads of sweat sat on Mira's upper lip; her eyes seemed larger than normal. That's what Harriet told her sister Christa, who had rung Harriet after Inga's call. Or part of it at least; the rest I just picked up bit by bit.

If Rosmarie knew that Inga was watching, a baffled Christa asked me after she had hung up the phone, why on earth had she kissed him? I stared at my mother in silence and the furrows above the bridge of her nose deepened. She looked at me coolly and said, "Oh. Do you think so? Well, I reckon you're letting your imagination get the better of you again." Then she bit her lip and turned away.

Inga had also said on the phone that she loved Peter and that she had come to think that the difference in their ages didn't matter. Unfortunately she had only realized this in the instant when he kissed her teenage niece, and she wondered whether she would ever be able to look him in the eye again after that. Harriet was concerned but helpless; at any rate Inga wouldn't talk to her. Christa calmed her sister down and advised her to talk to Peter. Inga said she needed some time to think everything through; she would spend the week in Bremen and then she intended to talk to him. My mother thought that sounded like a good plan, and the telephone conversation was at an end.

But much more would happen that week. After it had run its course it was all over between Aunt Inga and Peter Klaasen, and he had taken up a post somewhere in the Ruhr district.

Chapter XI

IN SPITE OF THE SHADE IT was now hot on the terrace. The sun was high in the sky; I padded back into the house to drink a glass of water. I went into Hinnerk's study, sat at the desk, and took a sheet of typewriter paper from a tall stack in the cupboard on the left-hand side. Then I took one of the perfectly sharpened pencils from the drawer and wrote an invitation to Max: *Tonight, at sunset, small reception, festive evening attire.* I added this at the end because I didn't want to be the only one all dressed up.

I slipped the piece of paper into a white envelope, wrote *Max Ohmstedt* on the front, put it in my bag, and went outside.

The heat hit me like a slap in the face. I cycled to Max's and put the letter in his letterbox. Other letters were in there, so he obviously hadn't emptied it today and was bound to get my message. But what if he already had something planned? Well, then he could just say no. I wasn't planning to cook a three-course meal.

I cycled on to the Edeka shop, bought some red wine and a box of After Eights for old time's sake. No one seemed shocked by my white ball gown. I put everything in my bag and returned to the house, ate some of what was in the fridge, and planned my evening's reception.

Where should we sit? On the steps outside the house, below the rose bush? Not festive enough, and it was visible from the road. On the terrace under the willow? Given what I wanted to talk to him about, the former conservatory was not the right place. In the copse? Too dark, too many spiky branches. In the chicken shed? Too poky, and anyway it would still smell of paint. In the orchard? In the middle of the lawn in front of the house? Or maybe inside?

I decided on under the apple trees behind the house. The grass was too tall, but there was plenty of garden furniture around to put things on. And behind the orchard the wide pastures began. I went into the barn and fetched Hinnerk's scythe. Why shouldn't I be able to do it, too? I tried to remember how my grandfather had wielded the scythe as he made his way easily and slowly through the falling blades of grass. But what had looked so easy was actually very arduous, and the heat didn't help things. Bravely I cut a rather uneven patch beside the large Boskoop tree in which Bertha and Anna had once had their hideaway. It looked less as if someone had tried to prepare a pleasant spot for a picnic and more like the site of a fight. It was, in fact, and the scythe had won. I hung the blunt tool back in its place. Only blankets would help now. I went upstairs, rummaged through the chests, and found a large patchwork rug, several coarse woolen blankets, and a golden-brown brocade curtain. I hauled them down the stairs as if they were the skins of animals I'd slain, dragged them through the barn and into the meadow at the back.

Those dower chests were wonderful. I went back and fetched a white broderie anglaise tablecloth. As I walked down the stairs again my gaze fixed on the bookshelf. The spines of the books were looking at me. I stopped. There wasn't any system; things just happened and sometimes the arrangement worked.

I took the tablecloth, grabbed a few dark green satin cushions with gold tassels from the living room, and went outside. The tablecloth fluttered on the rusty square folding table. I raked the freshly cut grass aside and spread out the rug. The woolen blankets came next and then the brocade curtain. I arranged the satin cushions on top and stretched myself out with delight in this wonderful nest and looked up into the tree. I couldn't see anything because I was gazing into the sunlight. I put my hand over my face.

When I awoke the sun was lower in the sky. Woozily I struggled up from the cushions. I couldn't remember ever having slept so much at any stage of my life before. But nor could I remember ever having scythed so much. As I lurched up the stairs I fancied I could hear an undertone of resignation—but not an unfriendly one—in their groaning.

I washed myself from head to toe at the basin, put up my hair, and slipped into the midnight-blue tulle dress that had once belonged to Inga. The layers of the skirt were made up of endless honeycombs of nothing, defined only by a blue thread. And the more these holes piled on top of one another, the more they concealed what was hiding beneath them. This dress had always been mine when I played with Rosmarie and Mira.

I thought of how we had met Mira. Max had been there, too. Rosmarie and I were playing ball out on the drive. We would throw it against the wall of the house and before it bounced back we had to clap: first once, then twice, then three times, and so on. The person who dropped the ball or forgot to clap the right number of times was the loser. We would also play it with other rules: having to turn right around between rebounds, say tongue twisters, and whatever else we could think of. All of a sudden, there in the middle of the drive was this girl with black hair and her little brother. Rosmarie knew who the girl was and where she lived. They went to the same school but the girl was one year above Rosmarie. It was clear that her brother was much, much younger than me, at least a year, you could see that right away. Poker-faced, the girl picked up little stones from the ground and started throwing them at Rosmarie. I was eager to see how my volatile cousin would react, and was outraged when she didn't do anything at all. She actually seemed flattered and showed the gaps in her teeth. She still had her pointy canines, but both her upper incisors were missing. This made her look even wilder and rather ferocious, too. I took a stone and threw it at the girl. But I only hit her little brother and he immediately started howling. So we let the two of them join our game.

I wondered what Max remembered. He must have been six at the time, his sister nine, me seven, and Rosmarie eight. Now we were twenty years older. But not Rosmarie, of course. She would remain almost sixteen forever.

I gathered my tulle dress and went downstairs to get some crystal glasses from the cupboard in the living room. Just as I was again mulling over what to do if he didn't come, if he had gone out with friends, perhaps to the cinema straight after work, I heard the doorbell ring. The glasses clinked in my hands. I went to the front door and opened it. Max was standing there, holding a bunch of marguerites. He was wearing a white shirt and black jeans and gave me a shy smile.

"Thanks for the invitation."

"Come in."

"You look . . . I mean, you're . . ."

"Thank you. Come on, give me a hand."

"What sort of invitation is that? Is it all self-service?"

But he appeared very happy as he followed me into the kitchen. I put the flowers in a vase and then placed it in one of his arms, the bottles of wine in the other. I retrieved the basket from the kitchen cupboard and filled it with glasses, plates, knives, cheese, bread, carrots, melons, chocolate, After Eights, and large linen napkins. And so we made our way through the barn to the orchard.

"Hey, what's that?" He obviously meant the blankets under the tree.

"I had to put all this stuff on the ground because underneath there's a patch of grass I hacked at with a scythe. But I've already had a delicious sleep on it today."

"I see. So you've been lying around here, stretching out your sinful body."

"For someone who races into a black lake in a panic at the sight of my sinful body, you've got nerve."

"Touché. Iris, I—"

"Shut up and pour the wine."

"Of course, madam."

We both took a few sips, and then we sat down beneath the apple tree.

"This is all a little frugal, but you're not here to eat."

Max gave me a sidelong glance. "No? I'm not?"

"Quiet. I need to talk to you."

"Fine. I'm listening."

"About the house. What happens if I don't want my inheritance?"

"We'd be better off talking about this in my office."

"But what would happen, in theory?"

"It would go to your mother and father. And then to you again at some point. Don't you want the house? I thought Bertha's decision to leave it to you was a stroke of genius."

"I love the house, but it's a difficult legacy."

"I can well imagine."

"Does your sister know I'm here?"

"Yes, I called her."

"What did she say?"

"Not a lot. She wanted to know if we'd talked about Rosmarie."

"No, we haven't."

"No."

"Would you like to talk about her?"

"I never got much of what was going on. I was younger than you and I was a boy. And perhaps you remember what things were like for us back then. I mean with my mother. After Rosmarie's death Mira was never the same again. She didn't talk to anyone anymore, not even my parents—especially not my parents."

"What about to you?"

"To me she did. At least sometimes."

"Is that why you stayed here? To mediate between your parents and your sister?"

"No, not at all!"

"I was only asking."

"Iris, you don't have a monopoly on love for the bog lake and the birchwoods, the lock and the rain clouds above cow pastures. Think about it for a second."

"You're a romantic."

"So are you. Anyway, what I wanted to say . . . about Mira. After your cousin died she didn't flip out, didn't take drugs, and didn't fall apart. She sat in her room all day long, working for her school-leaver's exams. She did the best math paper in the entire school, got top grades across the board, and studied law in record time. She's now got a PhD."

"In what? The Abortion Act? Paragraph 218?" That just slipped out.

Max's eyes narrowed. He glared at me. "No. Construction law."

An uncomfortable pause followed. Max stroked his face. Then he said, a little too casually, "I've got a short article about her here. It's more of an announcement that she's now a partner at this Berlin firm. It was in a legal newspaper a few weeks back. Do you want to see it?"

I nodded.

Max made a show of pulling out two torn out and double-folded pieces of paper from his back trouser pocket. So he had intended to talk about his sister all along. Did he have any other plans for this evening?

"There's . . . there's also a photo of Mira."

"A photo of Mira? Show me!" I grabbed the pieces of paper. And then I saw the picture.

Everything started spinning. The face on the paper came closer and then spun away again. I started to sweat. There was a pounding in my ears, an ugly metallic hammering. Please don't let me faint now, I thought; fainting would mean the end. I pulled myself together.

The face on the paper. Mira's face. I had expected a stylish haircut, black and gleaming like a helmet; a chic outfit, if not black then at least gray or even an eccentric purple—why not? Sexy and sophisticated, still the silent movie star.

But what I held in my hands was the picture of a beautiful woman with long copper-red hair and copper-red eyebrows, wearing a vanilla-yellow satin dress that shimmered almost as if it were gold. Without the thick eyeliner her eyes looked completely different. There was dark mascara on her lashes. She looked at me with a languid smile on her dark red lips.

I dropped the picture and gave Max a hostile stare. "What . . . what *is* that? Is she sick, or has she just got a sick sense of humor?"

"She let her hair grow and then dyed it red instead of black. As far as I know lots of people do it." Max returned my stare. Somewhat coolly, I felt. He hadn't yet forgiven me for the comment about Paragraph 218.

"But, Max! Just look at her!"

"Her hair's been like that for a while now. I mean, hair doesn't grow overnight. She stopped dyeing it black as soon as the thing with Rosmarie happened. Then she let it grow. She didn't dye it red till later."

"But surely you can see that . . ."

". . . she looks like Rosmarie. Yes, but I didn't see it till I got this picture. Maybe it's the golden dress, too. I haven't got a clue what it means. Why does it bother you so much?"

I didn't know exactly. All of us had had to come to terms with Rosmarie's death in our own way, hadn't we? Harriet had joined a sect, Mira had disguised herself. Maybe her way was more honest than mine. I shrugged and avoided Max's eye. The wine glistened dark in the large glasses. It was the color of Mira's lipstick. I didn't want to drink any more. It was making me stupid. And forgetful.

Mira and Max's mother, Frau Ohmstedt, had been a drinker. When her children came home from school and rang the bell, they could roughly calculate how drunk she was by the time it took her to get to the door and open it. "The longer it takes, the more smashed she is," Mira told us in a deadpan voice. Mira spent as little time at home as possible. Her parents disapproved of her black clothes, and on the day of her oral examination she moved into a friend's house, and soon after that to Berlin. It was different for Max. Because

Mira was so difficult he had to be considerate. He would clear away the empty bottles and cover his mother up if she couldn't make it to bed from the sofa.

Herr Ohmstedt was seldom at home; he built bridges and dams, and spent most of his time in Turkey, Greece, or Spain. In the past Frau Ohmstedt had gone with him; they had lived for more than three years in Istanbul. Frau Ohmstedt had loved it there: the Turkish bazaars, the parties and events organized by the embassy, the other German women, the climate, the lovely big house. When she fell pregnant with Max they decided to come back. After all, they hadn't planned to emigrate and they wanted to bring up their children in Germany. But what they hadn't realized was that it was much easier to go away than to come home.

Herr Ohmstedt had his work and needed to continue traveling, but Heide Ohmstedt remained here in Bootshaven. She didn't move into town for the sake of the children. She missed the close network of German expats. Here, everybody stayed in their houses, no one was interested in her. They called their indifference discretion and were proud of it. They called their impoliteness being direct, straightforward, or honest and were proud of that, too. Frau Ohmstedt gained the reputation of being eccentric, trying, hysterical, and superficial. She said things such as, "I couldn't give a damn about the people here, these 'hard nuts with their soft centers.'" In her opinion that was just an excuse for being permanently rude. Frau Ohmstedt soon became very lonely. She couldn't give a damn. She was particularly skilled at not giving a damn when she had had something to drink; then her abuse got keener and filthier.

Herr Ohmstedt was in despair. And helpless. And most of all, he wasn't there.

On the day when Max came home from school and found her lying on the terrace in her pajamas, with the temperature at minus seven degrees, she was taken to the hospital in an ambulance. She hadn't frozen to death. But she was admitted to a clinic and underwent four weeks of rehab. Max was sixteen at the time, Mira was already living in Berlin. The Wall was still standing then and Berlin meant far, far away.

Frau Ohmstedt did it by herself. She started working for the church, not because she had suddenly found Jesus, but because the parish network reminded her of the solidarity of the Germans in Istanbul. There were events, excursions, and lectures to organize, visits, women's groups, OAP functions, and walks. She tried to avoid spending too much time at home alone.

Now Max lived on his own in that house and went to the cemetery to get smashed. And he didn't have a girlfriend anymore. By all reckoning he ought to look rougher than he actually did, I thought, scanning his face for signs. Max watched me as I did this, and screwed up his eyes.

"So?" he asked. "Found anything?"

I blushed. "What? What do you mean?"

"Well, I can see that you're hunting for clues to implicate me as a codependent."

Now I turned a deep shade of red. I could feel it. "You're nuts."

"I'd do it if I were in your shoes." He shrugged and took a sip of wine.

I asked cautiously, "Why would you want to drink?"

"What do you want me to say? Should I say 'to forget,' hmm?"

I bit the inside of my cheek and looked away. All of a sudden I wanted him to leave. I wanted to decline my inheritance tomorrow morning and then go home. I didn't want this now. I didn't want to talk anymore, either. He should leave.

Max stroked his face again. "I'm sorry, Iris. You're right, I *am* nuts. I didn't mean to hurt you, you of all people. It's just that I was getting along fine here. In my life, I mean. There was nothing missing. It wasn't particularly exciting, but then I don't want exciting. I didn't want exciting. I wanted unexciting. No surprises. I do things right, I don't hurt anybody, nobody hurts me. I'm not responsible for anybody, nobody is responsible for me. I won't break anybody's heart and nobody will break mine. And then you come back here after God knows how many years. You pop up all over the place—and I mean that literally—and each time it scares me witless. And, if I'm being honest, I start to enjoy it! Even though I know that in a couple of days you'll be gone again, maybe for good. So now I can't sleep, I can't even cycle to the lake anymore without falling from my bike because of acute cardiac arrhythmia. Christ, I'm painting chicken sheds at night! Let me ask you: can it get any worse?"

I couldn't help laughing, but Max shook his head.

"No. No, no, no, no. Stop it. What do you really want?"

The sun had almost disappeared. From where we were sitting we could see the lime trees on the drive. The last of the green-golden light played on their leaves.

*

When Mira stood watching Inga watching Rosmarie kissing Peter Klaasen on the lips, she spilled all the lemonade. She put the two glasses, hers and the one for Rosmarie, beside her on the grass and, with the teeth inside her little red mouth, bit into the back of her right hand until it bled. There was a silver glint in Rosmarie's eyes when she told me that.

The day after the kiss, Mira went to the petrol station and waited until Peter Klaasen finished work. He had spotted her some time before and didn't want to talk to her. He couldn't stop reproaching himself and didn't dare speak to Inga for fear of losing her forever. Rosmarie had simply caught him off guard. He didn't want anything from her; he just wanted Inga.

Mira was leaning against his car when he came out to drive home. She said he ought to take her part of the way, she knew something that might interest him—it concerned Inga. What else could he do but open the passenger door? We'll go to your place, Mira had decided; he nodded. There he showed her into his room. Mira sat on his sofa and told him what he already knew: Inga had seen him kissing Rosmarie and didn't want him to come to the house ever again, neither for extra lessons nor for any other reason. Inga had also said that there was practically no one she despised more than the man who seduced his teenage tutee. Peter broke down. He put his head on the table and wept. Mira said nothing. She considered him with those eyes that seemed as if they were wrongly positioned on her face and thought of Rosmarie. Thought of how Rosmarie had kissed this man. Then she undid her black dress. Peter Klaasen looked at Mira without seeing her.

She was wearing black underwear; her skin was very white. She undid his shirt, but he barely noticed. When Mira placed her hand on his shoulder he thought of Inga and that this odd black-and-white girl before him was the final thing that linked him to her. Mira looked at his lips, which had touched Rosmarie's lips. Peter Klaasen realized far too late that Mira was still a virgin, but perhaps he hadn't wanted to realize it earlier. He drove her home; she was pale and silent. When Peter Klaasen got back to his room his eyes fell on the letter with the job offer near Wuppertal. When it had arrived he hadn't thought about it for a second. But now nothing was as it had been before. That same evening he wrote back and accepted. A week later he moved to Wuppertal. He never said another word to Inga.

Mira was pregnant. From her first time. And she hated Peter Klaasen. But he had left long ago. She told Rosmarie when they were sitting drinking apple juice in the kitchen. Everything was as it always was, the apple juice, the red oil-cloth, and yet nothing was as it had been before.

Rosmarie said, "You did it because of me, didn't you?" Mira just looked at her. Rosmarie said, "Get rid of it."

Mira remained silent and shook her head.

"Get rid of it, Mira," Rosmarie said. "You've got to."

Mira shook her head. She looked at Rosmarie, and the white stripe between her lower lid and brown iris was particularly visible.

"Mira. You've got to. You've got to!"

Rosmarie leaned over the kitchen table and kissed Mira firmly on the mouth. It was a long kiss. Both of them gasped for breath when Rosmarie sat back down. Mira was still silent, her face was very white and she had stopped shaking her head. She stared at Rosmarie. Rosmarie returned her gaze, opened her mouth to say something, but then threw her head back and laughed.

Rosmarie also laughed when she told me about it that evening. It was August, close to the end of my summer holiday. Although it was already past ten o'clock it was not quite dark when she came upstairs. We sat on the wide window seat in our room, which had been her mother's bedroom when she was a girl. Harriet's study was next door. She now used the second dining room as a bedroom, right next to the front door. This gave her a better chance of hearing if Bertha was roaming around downstairs.

"When did you talk about it? Just now?" I asked Rosmarie.

"No, a few days ago."

"And just now, were you at Mira's?"

Rosmarie gave a slight nod and turned away.

I froze and had no idea what to say. My mind was blank. Maybe I was hoping that Rosmarie was lying as payback for the argument we had had that day in the garden playing Eat or Die. I still resented her for slapping me. But deep down I knew that she had spoken the truth. If I'd had the choice I would have run to my mother and told her everything, but I couldn't do that. Not anymore.

Shortly afterward we went downstairs to say good night. Inga was there, too. The three sisters and their mother were sitting in the living room. Inga and Rosmarie hadn't said much to each other since the thing with Peter Klaasen. That evening, however, Inga got up and stood facing her niece. By now they were the same height. Inga raised both her hands and with a flowing movement stroked them from the crown of Rosmarie's head, over her untied hair, and down the sides of her arms. We could hear the electricity crackling throughout the room. Rosmarie didn't move.

Inga smiled. "Right. Sleep well now, child."

We went upstairs in silence. That night we told each other short tales about Rosmarie's father. I turned my back to Rosmarie and tried to fall asleep, deciding that I would tell my mother everything the next day after all. Sleep came slowly, but it did come in the end.

I dreamed that Rosmarie was standing behind me, whispering to me. I woke up. Rosmarie was kneeling behind me on the bed, whispering to me.

"Iris, are you awake? Iris. Wake up. Are you awake, Iris? Come on, Iris. Wake up. Come on! Iris. Please."

I had no intention of being awake again so soon. Rosmarie must have had a screw loose. First she hit me in the garden, then she did all those things with Peter Klaasen and then with Mira. And Mira did them with Peter Klaasen. I didn't want to know about any of it. I wished they would leave me in peace.

Rosmarie's whispers became more insistent, almost pleading. She should ask me quietly. I enjoyed being the one in control for once, even though I wasn't doing anything apart from pretending to be asleep. And I almost didn't have to pretend. She should go see Mira. Or the gray-haired math genius with the vase. In any event, I wasn't available.

Although I lay with my back to her I could feel the tension in Rosmarie. My body felt as if there were spikes growing through my skin from the inside. I couldn't go on lying motionless like this for long. I could sense that Rosmarie was on the verge of shaking me. Any second now her hand would grab my shoulder. Then I would have to scream at once. Rosmarie's hesitation was unbearable. Now I could feel her breath on my closed eyelids; she was bent over me. I summoned all my strength to avoid opening my eyes and blinking at her. A giggle rose inside me. It reached my throat and I was about to open my mouth and let it burst free when I realized from the movements of the mattress that she had turned away and was getting out of bed. I could hear her padding around the room. The long zip of a dress rasped when Rosmarie jerked it up—I found out later that it was the purple dress with the see-through arms. So she was going out somewhere? She really should go see Mira. Perhaps they wanted to meet to knit tiny black bonnets and tiny black coats. For babies with ice-gray hair.

I heard Rosmarie creep down the stairs. I was sure that, on hearing this noise, the entire household would be waiting for Rosmarie before she had even reached the last step. But nothing happened. I heard the creak of the kitchen door, which meant she was going out the side entrance. That was smart because the brass bell would surely have woken Aunt Harriet. Then silence.

I must have fallen asleep again because I gave a start when a hand touched my shoulder, gently but firmly. My first thought was that Rosmarie had come back, but it was my grandmother standing by the bed. Rosmarie wasn't there. I blinked sleepily at Bertha. She didn't usually come into the upstairs rooms during her nighttime wanderings. My mother was sleeping downstairs with her: surely she ought to have noticed something.

"Come," Bertha whispered.

Her white hair was loose. As she hadn't put in her teeth her mouth looked as if it had swallowed itself. I struggled to be patient with her.

"Grandma, I'll take you back to bed, okay?"

"Who are you then, young lady?"

"It's me, Iris. Your granddaughter."

"Is that so? I must be catching."

I stumbled down the stairs behind Bertha: she was fast. "No, Grandma. Not outside. To bed!"

But she had already taken the key from the hook, slipped it in the lock, turned it, and pushed down on the handle. The brass bell rang out like a gunshot through the house. My mother must have been sleeping deeply. Inga must have been upstairs.

Bertha stepped outside. It was warmer out here than in the old house. And brighter. The moon shone against a dark blue sky. It was large, almost full, and cast crisp shadows in the grass. Bertha walked down the steps and stopped abruptly, as if she had run into an invisible wall. She was looking at something that seemed to be in midair, in front of her rather than above. I stiffened. Her gaze usually wandered restlessly, as if it were seeking something to fix on to. But now she could see something. And I saw it, too. A dark figure was sitting high up in the willow. It was a while before I could make out Mira and Rosmarie. They were sitting so close to each other that you couldn't see their separate outlines. Then one figure broke away—it was Rosmarie—and slid slowly down from the bough of the willow onto the gently sloping conservatory roof. We weren't allowed to do that. It was an old conservatory. The roof was fragile; every other pane of glass was cracked or had partly come out of its steel frame. Rosmarie was balancing as she walked along the length of the metal frame. The sleeves of her dress puffed out in the night wind. Her arms glowed white. I couldn't call out. My mouth and tongue felt as if they were covered in dense gray cobwebs. Beside me, Bertha started to tremble.

Mira began screaming. It took me a few seconds to grasp that those sounds were really coming from a human being. For a moment I was distracted. When my eyes turned to Rosmarie once more she was looking straight at me. I was terrified. In the moonlight her eyes were practically white. She seemed to be smiling her predatory smile, but maybe her upper lip was simply curled above her incisors. Suddenly she threw her head back, lifted her foot from the metal frame and put it on the glass. Nothing happened at first, but then there was a crack. Mira fell silent. Reached out with her hand. Rosmarie took it.

And then it happened: Mira recoiled. Rosmarie had given her an electric shock. She lost her friend's hand. Crashing and cracking. A dull thud and an ear-piercing clatter that seemed as if it would never end. One pane of glass after another came away from its fixing and fell to the ground. Glass shattered on stone. Glass. The night air, bathed in moonlight, sparkled with slivers and shards. I screamed and ran indoors to get my mother and Harriet. When I reached the hallway all three sisters were already racing toward me. Inga wasn't wearing pajamas. We ran into the garden together. Mira had climbed down from the willow and was kneeling beside Rosmarie, screaming.

Rosmarie was lying on her back on the bright stones. The night wind toyed with the sleeves of her dress. Shards of glass lay all around her like crystals. A small trail of blood ran from her nose.

Harriet threw herself onto her daughter and tried to give her mouth-to-mouth resuscitation. My mother and Aunt Inga ran indoors and called an ambulance. It came and took Rosmarie; Mira and Harriet went with her.

When they had gone a dark pool of blood was left behind.

Rosmarie died of a brain injury. She had hardly lost any blood.

The pool of blood was Mira's.

That was how we found out about the abortion that Mira had undergone the day before.

Bertha had vanished. We began to look for her. Christa, Inga, and I were relieved to have something to do. We searched the garden together. She was standing beside the currant bushes.

"Anna, brock at me." She gave me an uncertain smile. "You're not Anna?"

I shook my head.

"Where is Anna? Tell me. I don't mersom what these balls are glicking." She pointed to the berries. "Where are we supposed to speen that? I mean, it won't be any better. Or what do you think? Go on, tell me. It bunts a shud. If we want to. Poor little me. Poor little me."

Bertha became even more agitated. She kept bending over to pick up fallen currants from the ground. "And the dancing just goes on and on. Here it's all smunge. We can't. Not as it was. The post's come. Tra-la-la. And that's it." She was crying.

She had also soiled her pajama bottoms. I wished I could cry, too. But I couldn't. I took Bertha's hand, but she got cross and snatched it back. I turned and walked away. Christa and Inga could sort this out. I couldn't. Bertha came behind me. When she saw Christa and Inga she waved to them and flung her arms around their necks. "Here are my mothers! What a joy! These lovely women."

Christa and Inga linked arms with Bertha and I followed on slowly behind. It was hard to make out who was actually supporting whom.

Since that night I've refused, every single night that's followed, to ask myself the following questions: What did Rosmarie want to tell me? Why did she want to wake me? Did she want to talk to me? Did she want me to talk to Mira? Did she want me to come with her? If so, where had she originally planned to go? To the lock, perhaps, or to the lake for a swim? Maybe just to the apple tree behind the house? Or maybe to see Aunt Harriet? Did she see Bertha and me standing there in the dark? Why didn't I call out to her? Why didn't she call out to me? Did she know about Mira's abortion? If not, then did Mira tell her that evening and was that why Rosmarie jumped—a life for a life? If so, did she perhaps want to tell me? If so, was she relieved? If so, had she got scared? And why had she climbed up there? Did she jump? Did she fall? Was it just a whim? Had she planned it? Did Mira let go of her by accident? Deliberately? Did she make Mira let go of her? What was that electric good-night gesture all about? Was it Inga trying to get her revenge? Did Rosmarie want to say good-bye to me? Did she want to tell me a secret? Did she want to make up with me? Did she want me to beg forgiveness? What would have happened if I had blinked? What would have happened if I hadn't acted all offended? What would have happened if I had crept down behind her? What would have happened if I had called to her outside? What did Rosmarie want to tell me that night? Why had she tried to wake me up? Was she always planning to go outside or did she go outside only because I refused to wake up? What did Rosmarie want to tell me? What was it, what? What did Rosmarie want to tell me? Why had I pretended to be asleep? What would have happened if I had giggled? What would have happened if I had blinked? What would have happened if I had listened to what she wanted to tell me? What did she want to tell me? What?

Chapter XII

MAX DIDN'T GO HOME. That night we made love under the apple tree.

When the sun came up we rode off together and swam in the lake. The water was still and cold, and where it wasn't silver it was black. I accompanied him back to his house, and he asked whether he could come over after work. I said yes.

As I tramped through the dewy grass to the orchard, I didn't notice anything at first. It wasn't until I stretched out on our makeshift camp and looked up into the tree that I saw it: the apples had ripened overnight. Heavy Boskoop apples with coarse green and red and brown skin were hanging from the branches. It was June. I got up, picked one, took a bite; it tasted sweet and sour, and the skin was slightly bitter.

I then went off to fetch a bucket and some baskets. On the way to the barn a thought crossed my mind and I took a detour to the currant bushes. But here everything was as usual. Only white and black ones.

I picked apples all day long.

It turned hot, the tree was big and it had lots of apples. I had leaned an aluminum ladder against the trunk. With the bucket and baskets and tubs I had found, there were also S-shaped metal hooks, one end of which you could hang over a branch. On the other you hooked the handle of the bucket. I went up and down the ladder many times with this bucket. It was hard work picking apples, but the tree made it easy for me. Its branches were strong and wide; I could stand and climb on them and so reach the fruit without too much difficulty.

Was this the apple tree that Bertha had fallen from before she got up, transformed into an old woman? I didn't know and it wasn't important, either. After Rosmarie's fall, Harriet fell apart. Inga looked for a place in a care home for Bertha. But it was almost two years before Harriet moved out of the house and found herself a flat in Hamburg. During that time Inga looked after her mother, bringing her home regularly in the afternoons so she could keep an eye on Harriet, too. My mother began traveling up to Bootshaven outside of my holidays. That was a relief, as I didn't want to go anymore. I paid a few brief visits during university vacations or I went to see Inga in Bremen. When she visited Bertha I didn't go with her, apart from the one occasion. I realized that this disappointed my mother and my aunts, but I couldn't help it.

Harriet didn't last long in Hamburg and she traveled to India for several months, where she took part in seminars at an ashram. It seemed to help her. The seminars were expensive; she moved into an even smaller flat and took on more work. At some point she started wearing the wooden-bead necklace with the Bhagwan's face hanging from it, and she began signing her letters with the name Mohani. But apart from that we couldn't see any major changes in her. There was none of the brainwashing that my mother and Inga had been worried about. She sometimes said things about spirituality and karma, but she had spoken about these sorts of things before. When Rosmarie was still alive. Christa said that whatever did Harriet good was good. For anybody who was incurable was also invulnerable.

Around this time, Inga walked past the practice of Friedrich Quast, purely by chance. She called her sister. A few days later, Harriet took the train to Bremen. She sat in the full waiting room. As she didn't have an appointment or a card, she had to wait until there was no one else left. She sat patiently. She wasn't waiting for much. And expecting nothing. Finally Dr. Quast himself beckoned her into his consulting room.

He must have seen a middle-aged woman with slightly shaggy henna-red hair. A flat, round face without any makeup. Wrinkles around the eyes and two deep indentations on either side of the bridge of her nose. He saw her clothes, the saffron, cinnamon, and turmeric colors she liked to wear, besides those of other spices. And her trainers. And he would have pigeonholed her instantly—old hippie, a touch esoteric, frustrated, probably divorced.

Without any curiosity he asked what had brought her here. She said her heart caused her pain. Day and night.

He nodded and raised his eyebrows, inviting her to say more.

Harriet smiled at him. "I had a daughter. She's dead now. Do you have a daughter? A son?"

Friedrich Quast glanced at her. He shook his head.

Harriet went on speaking softly, staring at him all the while. "I had a daughter. She had red hair like you and freckled hands like you."

Friedrich Quast placed his hands on the table. They had been in the pockets of his white coat the whole time. He said nothing, but his right eyelid began twitching ever so slightly when he met Harriet's gaze.

He cleared his throat. "I'm sorry. How old was your daughter?"

"Fifteen. Almost sixteen. Not a child, not a woman. She'd be just twenty-one now."

Friedrich Quast gulped. Nodded.

Harriet kept on smiling. "I was young and in love with a red-haired student. I'm very sad that he never had a daughter. And she didn't want to know where he was, even though I'd have given her every support if she'd wanted to find out. These things aren't always so difficult, you know. But it breaks my heart, because he'll never have this daughter. And it would break his, too, if he knew."

Harriet stood up, tears streaming down her cheeks. Friedrich Quast was ashen-faced. He just gaped at her, breathing fitfully. Harriet didn't seem to realize she was crying; as she left she said, "I'm sorry, Dr. Quast, I know you can't help me. You can't, but do you know what? I can't help you, either." Harriet went to the door.

"No. Don't. Don't go. What was her name? What was her name?"

Harriet looked at him. Her red eyes were expressionless. She would never tell him Rosmarie's name. He would never get even a piece of her.

She said, "I've got to go."

Harriet opened the door and closed it gently behind her. The receptionist eyed her mistrustfully as Harriet walked past her with hunched shoulders and a distracted nod.

The next time Inga was walking down that street, a few weeks later, she looked for his plaque, but it wasn't there. Another doctor had set up practice. Inga went in and asked after Dr. Quast at the counter. He doesn't practice here anymore, they said. You won't find him in this town any longer.

Inga stayed in Bremen. From time to time she had lovers—all of them good-looking, most of them a bit younger than her—but nothing serious. People kept her at arm's length, but she captured moments forever. In 1997 she won the German Portrait Award for the photographic series of her mother. She was also making electrostatics work for her. At Bertha's funeral she told me how a sudden temperature change had charged some film with static, and flashes had appeared on the images. This mistake had opened up a whole new world of possibilities and perspectives.

*

I had filled two washing baskets and a plastic tub with apples. I brought them into the house and left them in the kitchen. Should they be stored in the cellar or the barn? Where was it cooler and drier? For now, though, I'd leave them where they were, standing on the floor of the kitchen.

I leaned over a basket of apples and gazed at the black and white square stones. Maybe I would finally manage to do it today. But just as the first symbols began to emerge I heard footsteps behind me. Max came into the kitchen and stopped in his tracks when he saw me bent over the floor.

"Are you not feeling well?"

I looked up, bemused. "Yes, of course I am." I composed myself quickly and asked, "Do you know how to make apple puree?"

"I've never done it. But it can't be that difficult, can it?"

"Okay, so you don't. Do you know how to peel apples?"

"Yes I do, more's the pity."

"Excellent. Here's the knife."

"Where did these apples come from?"

"From the tree we slept under."

"I didn't sleep."

"I know."

"Apples? But it's . . ."

". . . June. I know."

"Seeing as you know everything, might you now explain it to me?"

I shrugged.

"Have you got the Tree of Knowledge growing in your garden? That'll push up the sale price of your house. So long as you don't reject your inheritance."

I hadn't thought about selling yet. I looked at Max; his mouth had narrowed. "What's up?"

"Nothing. I was just thinking that you'll be off again soon. That you might sell the house and never come back here again, or only in one hundred years in a wheelchair pushed by your great-grandson. He'll wheel you over to the cemetery and you'll throw an apple on my grave and mutter, 'Who was that again? What did he look like? Oh yes, I remember, he was the man who was forever ambushing me when I was naked!' And then a dry cackle will escape from your throat, still with its majestic poise. And your great-grandson will be terrified and let go of you at the very moment that he was about to push you up the steep bank behind the lock. And you'll roll backward and crash into the water, but at that very instant the lock gate will be opened and—"

"Max."

"Sorry, I always talk too much when I'm nervous. Right, come here and kiss me."

We peeled apples and cooked up twenty-three jars of puree. I couldn't find any more preserving jars. We had muscle cramps and calluses from turning the Mouli grater. Luckily there were two Moulis in the house, a big one and a small one, so we could both crank at the same time. We added some cinnamon and nutmeg to the puree, as well as three apple pips that I had peeled and chopped. The warm, sweet, earthy aroma of cooked apples filled every corner of the house. Even the beds smelled of it. It was a wonderful apple puree.

I spent the days that followed in the garden. I ripped out

mountains of ground elder and tetterwort, and carefully freed the stems of phlox and marguerites from the bindweed that was choking them. I dug up the columbines that had seeded themselves on the paths and replanted them in the beds. I pruned branches of lilac and mock orange so that the gooseberry bushes could get the sun again. I gently detached the small, delicate sweet-pea shoots from unreliable grass stems and guided them to the fence or tied them to a cane. The forget-me-nots had almost dried out by now, with only the odd twinkle of blue here and there. With thumb and forefinger I plucked them out by their thin stalks to scatter the seeds. I put my hand up into the wind and let the tiny gray grains fly away.

On the day I left, Max took me to the bus stop.

As the bus turned into the road I said, "Thanks for everything."

He tried to smile, but it slipped. "Forget it."

I got on and found an empty seat. When the bus moved off with a jolt, my body sank heavily into the backrest.

Epilogue

I'M SITTING AT HINNERK'S DESK, looking out at the yard. The lime trees are bare. Now I know what the garden looks like in winter. I've made it winter-proof eleven times, laying branches of pine over the beds, coir matting around the tender plants, pruned back roses and shrubs. In February the meadow in front of the house is full of snowdrops.

On the desk are the notes of a Bremen architect and essayist who documented the events and phenomena of the Bremen art scene in the 1920s before emigrating to America. I'm editing his unpublished works.

*

Carsten Lexow died a year after Bertha. He simply keeled over. With pruning shears in his hand.

My son is skateboarding between the limes on the drive with his friends. I have to restrain myself from knocking on the window to tell him to pull his trousers up higher and do up his coat. But I won't be able to hold out for long. It's freezing.

Over the past few days I've been arranging the rooms upstairs for my parents. My father has decided to move away from southern Germany because my mother's homesickness has got out of hand. She's weeping a lot and eating little. She's closing herself off.

She's forgetting.

Sometimes she can't remember whether she has cooked or not. Sometimes she even forgets how to cook. Maybe it will be easier for her here in the house, but I don't think so. Nor do I believe that my father thinks so, either.

I've still not seen Mira yet, even though she's part of the family now, but we call each other from time to time. Max has more contact. She's still a partner in the law firm and for the past eleven years has been living with a female teacher in an old Berlin tenement flat. When I talk to her on the phone neither of us mentions Rosmarie. We focus so hard on not talking about her that we can hear her breath on the line. And the rustling of the night wind in the boughs of the willow tree.

Acknowledgments

Thanks are due to Birgit Schmitz and Katja Weller. I should also like to offer my warmest thanks to Anke Hagena and Otfried Hagena, Gerd Hagena, Erika Thies and Christiane Thies. Thanks and love go to Christof Siemes, Johann and Mathilda.

About the Author

KATHARINA HAGENA, born in 1967, studied English and German literature in Marburg, London, and Freiburg, before lecturing at Trinity College Dublin and the University of Hamburg. Her first book, *What Are the Wild Waves Saying? Waterways Through Joyce's Ulysses,* was published in 2006. *The Taste of Apple Seeds* is her first novel. Her second novel *On Sleep and Disappearing* came out in 2012. She currently lives in Hamburg.

EAGLE VALLEY LIBRARY DISTRICT
P.O. BOX 240   600 BROADWAY
EAGLE, CO 81631   (970) 328-8800